WAR STORIES

J. J. ZERR

WAR STORIES

iUniverse books may be ordered through booksellers or by contacting:

iUniverse
1663 Liberty Drive
Bloomington, IN 47403
www.iuniverse.com
1-800-Authors (1-800-288-4677)

ISBN: 978-1-5320-0612-8 (sc)
ISBN: 978-1-5320-0613-5 (e)

Library of Congress Control Number: 2016916338

Print information available on the last page.

iUniverse rev. date: 11/07/2016

For Roy and Tom and for Jerry and his family.

For wimmin'.

Even in paradise, Adam couldn't get along without one.
Getting along with wimmin' is a struggle—sometimes.
But then I think about
my One and Only Squeeze, my daughters, my mom.
Without having had them in my life, I
cannot imagine who, what, where,
or why I'd be.

Thanks, as always, Karen; the Bubbas and Bubbettes from Coffee and Critique; and Margo, Plumgrace, Holly S., and the semianonymous but totally excellent editors at iUniverse. Remaining faults are all mine. None are theirs.

There is an appointed time for everything …
A time of war, and a time of peace.
—Ecclesiastes 3, the New American Bible

We offer each other Christ's peace in church,
but it doesn't even last till we get out of the parking lot.

—Karen Zerr

Contents

---

* Published previously in *Well Versed, Literary Works 2013* by the Columbia Chapter of the Missouri Writers' Guild (CCMWG). Published here with permission of CCMWG.

† Published previously in *Our Voices*, by the Military Writers Society of America in 2013.

What Kind of Man Are You?

My name is Joe Bob. What I am is a pilot.

Some folks may see me as other things. But I'm talking about if all the skin-deep stuff is stripped off me and I look in the mirror, what do I see? A pilot.

Pop didn't talk about what he was, except with his World War II buddies. Even as a kid, I noticed how alike they looked, Pop and his buddies. Tall, hair cut short, faces tanned. Slender to the point of being skinny. Pop's flight suit—zoom bag, he called it—hung on him as if he were a scarecrow with nothing but naked sticks to cover. Pop didn't say much about anything else either, except when he got together with his -17 cronies. Then he spewed words like an oil well that had been drilled deeper and deeper, and just short of the foreman giving up and moving his roustabouts someplace else, it came in a gusher. Listening to Pop and his friends, I figured out what he was—a B-17 pilot who had flown twenty-five missions over Germany.

After the war, he found flying jobs and eventually started a crop dusting business, but none of those things changed what he was. The way I looked at it, if God or the devil had taken a corkscrew and pulled the B-17 pilot and twenty-five missions out of him, it would have been like pulling the sticks out of a scarecrow. There'd be nothing left of him but an empty zoom bag piled on the ground.

Pop taught me to fly, and I dusted for him during my high school years. He and the other three pilots he employed flew a lot of missions in the early-morning hours—in the dark. The air was still and didn't blow the chemicals to hell and gone. He wouldn't let me dust at night, though I could have.

"You log two hours of night time every month," he told me, punctuating his words with that skank eye of his, though as rarely as he talked, he didn't need to embellish his words, "or I'll kick your ass."

Halfway through high school, I had fifty hours of nighttime in my logbook. I asked Pop if I could dust at night.

"No."

"Why not?"

"Y'ain't ready."

"Well, when the hell will I be?"

He skank-eyed me and walked away. No point in bringing that up again. So I dusted in the dawn's early light.

Then in the summer after my senior year, and two weeks before I was set to leave for college and the US Navy ROTC program, Pop surprised me when he pulled a chair up next to my desk in the ops shed. It was dark out, and he was flying that morning. He plopped onto a battered metal fold-up chair and looked at his big callous hands as if he hadn't seen those strange things before.

"Joe Bob," he said to his hands, "so many guys didn't survive twenty-five missions. I did." Then he looked me in the eye and really surprised me. I didn't know the man talking to me. "The hell of it is—all those who died, I feel like I ought to remember their names. But I don't. I can't even call up their faces anymore. What I do see is bombers blowing up or wings coming off and bits and pieces of aluminum raining out of the sky trailing orange fire and black smoke. Sometimes there were parachutes. Sometimes not."

That was a boatload of words from him. If he'd said a few of those to Mom, she might have stayed living with us. I didn't think he was done talking, but he was.

He stood up abruptly, spun on his heel, walked out through the door across the ramp, and climbed into his plane. After dusting a peach orchard to kill some vermin imported from some foreign country, he flew into power lines. Killed himself. He'd found out the day before he had cancer.

His B-17 buddies showed up the day before the funeral. One of them, Ralph, put his little hand on my shoulder and looked up at me. I'm a good two inches taller. He probably didn't weigh one seventy, so I had him there by fifty pounds. He told me I had to deliver the eulogy—that it was my duty as his son.

Contemplating your hanging on the morrow is supposed to concentrate your mind. So does eulogizing your father.

We held the funeral in Galveston, in the church we'd gone to when Mom was still with us. In attendance were the four -17 guys, the three pilots from Pop's business, and the three old women who never missed Mass on Sunday or a funeral on any other day of the week.

I told them what Pop was. "And for the longest time, I thought that was all there was to him—you know, like there was no real man wrapped around the *what* of him. I did get a glimpse at the real man, the *who* of him, the day he died. I wish I could have seen more. But I didn't. I always admired the hell out of him.

"Pop was a man of few words. I think he'd admire it of me, if I were that way too."

As I walked back to my pew, I saw the women in the back of church, all three of them, dabbing lace-edged hankies at their noses under the gauzy veils. They always sniffled at funerals.

Ralph had a tear running down his cheek. I hadn't expected to see that.

⚬━✦━⚬

I buried all of that with Pop. I never thought on it again, about the who and what of a man or what makes old women, and men, weepy. Well, for thirty some years, I didn't think on it. Now that I'm in my forties—early forties, well, midforties—it has come back to me. Thinking about the *what* and *who* of a person. Of me.

The *what* was easy. Me, I'm a pilot. A stick and throttle jockey, a driver of airplanes. The who I am, though? After watching other men try to tell people who they were, I've concluded a man is not a good judge of his own character if he gets to thinking on it. Who a man is is for other people to figure out.

I decided to tell my story so that maybe someday, some people will know who I am. Actually, there's one person I hope understands the who of me.

My story starts in 1976. It could start earlier, but I don't care to talk about Vietnam—the war we lost. Though I sure as hell didn't lose my part, the stink of losing hangs on me like when I step on a dog turd and don't realize it until I get in my pickup. The year 1976—that was when BUPERS, the US Navy's Bureau of Personnel, who I love about as much as I love losing wars and stepping in dog's doings, sent me to be the flight deck officer on the USS *Marianas*. Back then, an aircraft carrier flight deck was not a place for sissies. My bet, it's still that way.

On a flight deck, lots of things can kill a person or, worse, maim him. Jet exhaust, now and then, blows an inattentive sailor over the side, or it rolls him down the rough, nonskid deck, flaying clothing and skin off at every tumble and then blows him over the side—bleeding. Carriers dump a lot of garbage. Sharks love garbage. And bleeders. Occasionally, a careless maintenance man is sucked down an intake, which turns out some kinda ugly. Once in a while, a landing plane crashes against the steel cliff at the back end of the boat and spews shrapnel and burning fuel down the length of the deck, scything away and frying anyone in its path. No sir, not a place for sissies.

But of course that's exactly what the Bureau of Personnel sent me to crew up my flight deck during a Mediterranean cruise. Sissies. My seventeen-year-old recruits were pansy-asses who couldn't do anything but grow pimples.

A flight deck officer didn't get to choose his pansy-asses. Neither did he get a lot of time to turn them into hard-asses.

The wusses needed to function in the middle of a couple dozen jet engines packed close together and howling like pissed-off banshees. They needed to understand they sure as hell wouldn't hear danger coming. Their heads on a swivel, they needed to look around, continuously. That was the only way a man could save his ass on the deck of a flattop. Flight deck officers hated to see their people get killed or hurt. It was a regular pain in the butt to train up new ones. And there was paperwork.

Once a kid got over fouling his skivvies just being on the flight deck during operations, I could teach him how to move planes from parking spots to cats, which is short for catapults, without dinging them or losing one over the side. Time was sacred; that was another thing they needed to learn. If a launch was scheduled for 0900, then number one cat better fire exactly at the instant that the second hand overlapped Mickey's big hand pointing straight up. The other three cats fired *Kaboom. Kaboom. Kaboom.* Reload the cats and get twenty planes in the air in seven minutes, and as the last cat fired off the bow, the first plane landed from the previous launch.

During my indoctrination talk, I gave them one of my *herds of words to the not totally stupid*. They went like this:

"Do not be the guilty bastard who screws up the timing."

"Propellers and jet intakes want to eat you and shit you out as spaghetti sauce."

"Sharks following our flattop hope like hell jet exhaust blows you overboard."

I, Lieutenant Joe Bob Norgood, was a good flight deck officer. Packed with modesty, that statement. Training the pansies turned out to be a special talent. Besides having a way with words, I made the kids more afraid of me than they were of intakes, jet exhaust, crashes, or sharks. It wasn't that simple though. The danger was turning them from sissies to stupid fearless, which pretty much happened to my first batch. In that business, you lost a few, you know? I adjusted. I developed finesse, a deft touch.

I became Lieutenant Buddy-Buddy, Mr. Nice Guy. But cocooned inside was a volcano, not a *wuss* volcano like Kileauea, Etna, or Vesuvius. I'm talking Krakatoa. The thing blows, and where a honking island once was, nothing remains but a smoking hole in the ocean. Stunning in its sudden violence. My teenagers never knew when the eruption was going to happen. Some days, I'd screw them up with Mr. Nice Guy all day. They'd think, *For sure he'll go off tomorrow.* At the end of the next day, just when my bepimpled minions were convinced it wasn't going to happen, I'd Krakatoa 'em.

Finesse. Deft touch. Like that, see?

So anyway, one day on the USS *Marianas*—

Oh, one other thing. On a flattop, half the crew was assigned to the carrier—ship's company they were called. The air wing made up the other half. Air wing they were called. Ship's company hated the air wing. Without the 2,500 wing nuts, a carrier was the nicest, most pleasant boat to sail on. Workdays were four, five hours long. You had all the time in the world to eat chow and watch movies—skin flicks if that floated your boat. But then the assholes showed up with their eighty-eight airplanes. Jesus! The workday immediately extended to twenty hours, the ship became oily and dirty, and the chow lines were long all day and night. And the arrogant pricks thought the ship and ship's company were there to serve them and their almighty airplanes! Pricks!

Actually, at the time I got that dicked-up ship's company tour, courtesy of the even more dicked-up BUPERS, I was a pilot and had made two carrier cruises. There never was a point to bitching to BUPERS. They gave a you a gig, you pitched in, and you got the job done. The way it worked, a pilot checked into the ship, and by some sort of spiritual osmosis, by his second day, he was ship's company, and the air wing sucked. The fact that he had just come from the air wing had no power to alter any of the preceding.

Back to that day on the *Marianas*, we were in the Mediterranean working cyclic ops, which meant we launched twenty planes every ninety minutes and recovered the ones from the previous go. It was nineteen minutes before the third launch, and we had one of those rare occurrences. All the planes were ready—four minutes ahead of time! Across the flight deck, there wasn't a single sailor anywhere scramble-assing to get some last piece in place. This was rare, a thing to savor, and I did. In that handful of minutes, there was time to appreciate my boys. I thought about them, what they'd been like when they'd first come up and what they were capable of after a few months of experience. They worked with the tiniest of margins, hundreds of gallons of jet fuel inside thin-skinned jets, tons of explosives, and an urgently ticking clock. They performed perfectly, even in miserable weather and on black-assed nights. They were good kids, and it was good to take three minutes every month or so to appreciate them.

I should have known. Stop and bend over to smell a rose, and a pit bull chomps off a pound of your butt.

We were seconds away from sending the first jet to the cat when I heard an S-3 engine sound weird and then shut down. It turned out an air wing kid had stood up right in front of an S-3 intake and was sucked in.

An S-3 was a new antisub plane. It had an engine with honkin' big, first-stage fan blades under each wing, some kind of aerodynamic design shit that gave it good fuel specs. And those blades, well—

I hadn't seen the mishap. I saw people running toward the starboard side of the ship, and I wondered, *Now what have those dipshit wingnuts done?* A guy lay on the deck, blood puddled under him, blood splattered on the side of the S-3 above him.

The kid was dead, no question.

I ran to the crowd and jerked kids' arms. "Get back to work. We got a launch to make." I pushed some of them hard in the back and kicked some others hard on the ass. I told two of my sailors to move the dead guy down to the hangar bay and turn him over to a quack. Then I hollered into my radio, "Keep those goddamned planes moving to the cats! Keep your heads outta your asses, but move those planes."

My flight deck chief, he was a good one. He grabbed arms and hollered into the ear cups of peoples' helmets. The planes moved again, the way they should.

My guys had the dead kid strapped to a wire basket stretcher.

"Take him to the aft aircraft elevator on the starboard side," I hollered into Seaman Sanchez's ear.

I radioed another two of my crew. "Charge a two-and-half-inch fire hose and spray the blood over the side."

Two planes aft of the S-3, an air wing guy stood in front of an F-14. He bent over and puked on the deck. He'd been able

8

to handle the dude getting killed. But hosing the gore of the decapitation over the side like the remains were nothing more than a big *splop* of seagull shit and going on with the business of launching was too much for him. The fire hose did him in. He wiped a hand across his mouth and walked forward toward the island.

I stopped him and hollered, "Get back to your goddamned job."

"What the hell kind of man are you, shithead, sir?"

Puke spit hit my face, and I could smell it on his breath.

He jerked his arm free and started forward again.

Throwing his sorry ass over the side occurred to me, but I let him go. The air wing sissy didn't belong on my flight deck.

What kind of man are you? It wasn't the first time I'd heard that question.

My next assignment was to fly airplanes, my natural calling, rather than bein' a dumb ass ship's company puke. Two years—it was a long time to be away from flyin'. Six months of training would be required to get back into it. Halfway through the flight refresher course, I met this girl at a softball game on the base at Naval Air Station Lemoore, California.

As she watched the game, her face shone with a combination of untouchable, angelic innocence and the magnetic invitation of a pole dancer who pulled fives and tens out of a guy's wallet. She was fry-your-eyes gorgeous with a face lifted off Michelangelo's Pieta in St. Peters. Her ponytail begged a man's fingers to fondle the blond tresses. She wore a white sleeveless blouse and shorts. Her arms and legs belonged on a Barbie doll. She could have been a Barbie, except she wasn't overly endowed. No, she was perfect. She was absolutely beautiful. Everybody else thought so too and that they wouldn't have a chance. So they didn't try. Joe Bob said what the hell, walked over, and sat next to her.

We hit it off. Come to find out, she was a sailor, a supply clerk. Male officers and female enlisted—there was supposed to be distance between them. We saw each other but kept it quiet. Hell, I had never before been interested in a particular girl. I liked her.

During high school, there were drive-in movies. Later, bars served as one-nighter supermarkets. With those, who needed entangling alliances? But then I met Amanda Sue at the ballgame.

Two weeks later, we got hitched. We still didn't tell the navy. As long as she didn't get knocked up, it'd work. I bought a house on the edge of town.

Flying was good. Married life was good. I even started thinking about the future. Cheap farmland was available. There were guys who'd rent if I bought. I had money from Pop's estate. I bought. The rent paid off the loan plus a bit. There was a future out there in front of Amanda Sue'n me. Maybe a L'il Joe Bob Jr. too.

Near the end of training, my class was going to deploy to Naval Air Station Fallon, Nevada. NAS Fallon was ringed with practice bombing ranges. There, we'd fly twice a day and knock out the whole bombing syllabus in a third the time it'd take flying from Lemoore. I was supposed to ride up in a transport plane. The instructor pilots flew our bomber planes. Being a student again sucked in many ways. But what could I do? I went with the flow.

If we met our schedule, we'd get half of the next Saturday and all day Sunday off. A couple of us were going smoothbore hunting in the mountains around Reno. At the transit terminal on the base, I was turning my gear over to an enlisted baggage handler when I noticed the flint on my gun had broken. And I hadn't brought a spare.

I told my buddy, Dog Lips, my problem and that I had to go

home to get flints. "Don't let them leave without me," I said. "I'll be back in forty-five minutes."

"We're leaving in thirty-five minutes. Shit, man. I'm just a lieutenant junior grade. I can't stop a navy transport."

"Just hold the plane. For five minutes. That's all I need."

I got lucky racing home. No cops. At my house, a yellow Camaro was parked in the drive. Amanda Sue didn't have any friends with a car like that.

Opening the front door, I heard the sound of passion coming from the bedroom. Easing the door shut, I walked across the carpet. The bedroom door was open. I saw a guy's white, hairless buttocks pumping up and down. Amanda Sue's face, on her pink pillow, was turned away from me. She was moaning.

I wasn't pissed off, which surprised me. *Shouldn't I be?* A couple of optional actions rolled through my head. A Dirty Harry .44 magnum lay in the drawer of the bedside stand. They were doing the deed on her side of the bed, which was thoughtful, and were occupied right enough. I could get the gun and they wouldn't even notice. Kill them both? Both with one bullet? One bullet each? Kill just him? Just her?

Should I kill 'em when it just doesn't matter all that much?

Questions were piling up, and nowhere was an answer to be found, except one. It was high damn time to do something.

My Buck Knife. I never left home without it. Mr. Buck jabbed the guy's right buttock on his up stroke.

The guy rolled off her squealing like a half-killed pig. He stopped squealing, grimaced, put his hand back there, and studied the blood on his palm for a moment. Then he looked up at me. He was angry as all get out. He was in my bed, doing the deed with my wife, and he was mad at me! He began lobbing *sons of bitches* and *f* words at me. I'd always thought that *f* word showed a lack of class and breeding.

In the bathroom, I grabbed her pink towel and threw it at him. He was bleeding some. It wasn't bad though, considering what me and Mr. Buck Knife could have done.

"Sit on that in the car," I told him. "That wound needs pressure. You'll make it to the base hospital with twenty minutes to spare before you bleed to death."

He was holding the towel back there with both hands. He'd quieted and was glaring at me. I opened the drawer and pulled out the magnum, checked the cylinder for loads, and snapped it shut.

"Gather your clothes, Commander."

I recognized him. He was the supply officer on the base. Amanda Sue worked for him. He was a rather distinguished-looking dude. A six-footer, he was slender and had thick, gray hair and a gray moustache. Being naked diminished him some. His bloody butt didn't help much neither. Even with that, his face still wore that my-shit-don't-stink look. His blue eyes found the big hole in the barrel staring back at him.

He held up a bloody hand to forestay me shooting him. "Lieutenant—"

I cocked the hammer. "Open your mouth again, and I will blow your head off." Dirty Harry woulda said "clean off," but I figured I didn't need Dirty's clean. I gestured with the gun.

Sitting on the towel on the bed, he slipped his shirt on; then he stood to pull up his pants. Blood trickled down his leg. At least it wasn't a spurter. Then he pressed the bloody towel to the outside of his pants, gathered the rest of his clothes, and left.

Guess he thought showing up at the main gate in uniform would go over better than being naked. The gate guards wouldn't see his bloody butt.

"What kind of an animal are you?" Amanda Sue asked.

I pointed the pistol at her.

"Joe Bob, wait. We can—"

"Shut. Up."

I have a pretty fierce evil eye, I've been told. She shut up. I watched the doorway to see if the commander was going to come back to argue about anything. He made a little noise fumbling around in the living room. The front door slammed. A car door slammed. A car with grumble mufflers cranked up—manly sounding, those glasspacks.

Loud grumble. Grumble diminishing. Silence.

She had the sheet pulled up over her chest. Modesty—after screwing Mr. F Word Aristocrat. In my damn bed!

I pointed the pistol up and let the hammer down.

"Amanda Sue, here's what you're going to do. Move out, like right now. Find a lawyer. Get us a divorce. You get nothing of mine—not my house, not my furniture. Don't even think about my pickup. You get your clothes and the pink bath towels."

Her blue eyes grew big under the blond bangs. Then she squinted. A fierce frown bloomed. "What kind of a f—— animal are—"

I cocked and fired the magnum into the pillow next to her, on my side of the bed. It was my damn blue pillow.

She put her hands over her ears and opened her mouth. I didn't hear the first part of her scream. The noise of the shot in the bedroom deafened me and made my ears ring. But she kept the thing going long enough that I heard the tail end. She'd dropped the sheet, raising her hands over her ears. I didn't even appreciate the view.

"Move," I said.

She did.

Her butt was a lot cuter than the old fart's. I appreciated that a little bit.

I think of those four buttocks from time to time. I have that from two months of marriage.

I hustled back out to the base and arrived just as the transport lifted off at the far end of the runway.

Phooey. That was an f word I could tolerate.

Over the years I'd learned the slings and arrows of outrageous fortune; the vicissitudes of life flung a lot of crap in front of a man. He couldn't let it bother him. No, sir. My philosophy: Do not let your chin drop. Find a way. Keep going forward until your heart stops, your eyes go dim, and you fall off your legs.

Base operations.

I hustled out the door and into the truck and cranked it up. The damn thing purred.

Phooey. Need me a manly muffler!

After parking in the admiral's parking spot, I ran inside and leaned on the counter. "Any other planes flying up to Fallon today?" I asked a sailor's back. He was bent over a fax machine.

He stood up and turned. He was a she and some kinda ugly, which was the only kind of female sailor dicked-up BUPERS oughta let in my navy.

She pointed up to a grease board with the departures listed on it. There was one entry. An airplane from my training squadron would take off in forty-five minutes.

I started to leave, turned, and threw her a casual salute. "Thanks."

She blushed.

Maybe an ugly one would be loyal.

Joe Bob, a voice said, *forward's t'uther way.*

I heeded the voice, being mature and all.

I drove to the squadron and ran up to the second deck of the hangar, lugging my gear. Butt Chin, an instructor pilot, was suiting up.

"Butt Chin, you're going up to Fallon?"

He nodded.

"Flying a two-seater?"

He shook his head.

"You got a baggage blivet on the bird?"

A baggage blivet was a three-hundred-gallon fuel tank modified to carry airplane parts and luggage, beer too, on very rare and totally sanctioned occasions. It was suspended from a bomb rack under the plane.

"I do. It's not full. You got something you want me to haul up for you?"

At 1700, Butt Chin and me walked up the sidewalk to the officer's club at Naval Air Station Fallon. I told BC he didn't need to buy a beer the whole time we'd be in Nevada.

"I'll have the bartender open a tab." Second thoughts, prudent second thoughts occurred. "I'm going to check the tab every day. I find out you've gone on a generosity binge and started buying rounds for everybody, I'll cut you off."

"Hell, man, you owe me. But two weeks of free drinks, it's just the right thing to square us. I'm not going to abuse the gift horse. You know me."

I wrapped my paw around his biceps and spun him to face me. "That's why I'm telling you, you abuse this good deal I'm setting up for you, I'll rip your right arm off and beat you to death with the bloody stump, which means I won't owe you no more."

I squeezed his arm till he winced. Then I pulled open the door for him, and happy noises spilled out.

It got quiet as the revelers paused to see who was coming in. After the bright late of the afternoon sun outside, faces were not distinguishable in the dim smoke-filled bar. The skipper's voice we recognized though.

"Butt Chin, Joe Bob, you two dumb shits, come with me."

The skipper headed toward a side room off the main bar. Damned smoke watered my eyes. Somebody'd bought cigars. Married guys just went bonkers when they got away from home for a couple of weeks. That thought gave me a twinge of nostalgia. It lasted a couple of microseconds.

We followed the skipper into the room. He closed the door behind us and glared at a spot on the floor to my right. His lips were open in a snarl. I could see his teeth. I could hear him breathing through his mouth.

"Uh, Skipper—"

The skipper's head snapped up, and his eyes stopped Butt Chin. It reminded me of a time I'd been hunting grouse in the desert over at China Lake. A little, long-tailed mouse scampered into striking range of this Mohave green rattlesnake sunning close to where I sat. I got along fine with snakes, but that mouse stopped in its tracks and quivered, too scared to move. Butt Chin's Adam's apple bobbed. His big, scared eyes stared into the skipper's ferocious glare, just like that mouse meat.

The skipper and BC were the same size—five eight or nine, about one forty or so, about what I use for dumbbells working out.

"I want to make sure I got the story right. Tell me. No BSing now. Did you give Joe Bob a ride up here in a baggage blivet?"

BC shifted from one foot to another. Finally, he nodded. "But we planned it out, sir. I didn't go above ten thousand feet. We disabled the bomb rack so it couldn't be dropped accidently."

"Planned it out! Planned it out, did you? Jesus Christ! You're an instructor pilot. I expect you to keep these numb nut students safe, not endanger their goddamned lives. Especially, I expect my instructors to not let students idiot them down to their level. You're in hack."

Hack meant Butt Chin would be confined to his room in the

bachelor officer quarters. Someone would bring him his meals. There'd be no beer. The tab wasn't going to cost me a cent. So many clouds had silver linings.

The skipper swiveled his head slowly to me and hit me with his predator eyes. I could play poker. I didn't let my face say anything.

"What the hell kind of"—the skipper was another *f* worder— "excuse for a naval officer are you? The lieutenant commander promotion list just came out. Your name's on it. No way in hell I'm letting you get promoted. Not going to happen."

He gave me two choices.

The Bureau of Personnel was dicked up, but they moved real fast when a majorly pissed-off commanding officer cattle prodded them in their bureaucratic asses. My resignation came back approved quicker than grass goes through a goose.

Which was how I got back into the crop dusting business.

I asked a guy named Albert Mendoza for a job. According to him, his family had lived in the San Joaquin Valley for a hundred fifty years. Albert acted snooty. Aristocratic. Reminded me of the supply commander. He pissed me off.

"So you're a dryback?"

I asked politely, but Albert was upset. He ranted and waved his arms. I didn't understand any of it. I only speak American.

After a bit, he calmed down and told me I was "this close, this close" to being fired before being hired.

I did want a job, so I said, "I meant no disrespect, Mr. Mendoza. Hell a … your people, one of them does the work of two or three white men for a lot less pay. And they take their money with gratitude, whereas your white guy will bitch it's not enough. How about I call them LBWM?"

"What is LBWM?"

"Little brown working machines."

He had to think about that for a while. Finally, he shook his head. "No. It is so simple. You are a goddamned American. We are Mexican, goddamn it. Same thing."

It sure as hell was not the same thing. America was a place people tried to get into. Mexico was a place people tried to get out of. I wanted to win the argument, seeing's how I was right, but I wanted a job "this" much more.

Not a problem for Joe Bob—Mr. Sensitive-to-the-Feelings-of-Others.

At any rate, Albert hired me. I worked hard for him. Most of his duster pilots only did that one job. I did anything needed doing. Dig a ditch during the windy times of day? Sure. Fly at night and early morning? You bet. I made good money. Bought more farmland.

I began a fourth year with Albert. It turned out, he was a good guy. He called me his BWWM, big white working machine. He always laughed his ass off when he said it, and I liked him. The work was getting a little stale, though. I'd never had a job last so long. In the navy, you moved every two years.

The way we did the dusting, one guy flew the plane. Another guy, a Mexican goddamn, drove a pickup at the end of the field. The pilot laid a swath of spray, cut the juice off, and turned around as the driver moved the vehicle to mark where the pilot should start his next run. I got to thinking, I could do a touch-and-go landing on the roof of the truck.

The next morning, I made four passes over the spotter and decided to try it. The driver stood next to the hood and watched me approach. At the last minute, he realized I was lower than normal and dove into the ditch beside the field.

I kissed the roof so lightly with my left wheel I didn't even dent it. The black rubber streak was a bitch to get off though. I cleaned the truck and, since I didn't speak his language, made a lips zipped signal to the driver, punctuating the message with my evil eye.

The next morning, I had the same spotter. I figured his lips were still sealed, and I kissed the wheels of my landing gear on the top of his truck every time I turned around, which was somewhere near twenty times.

Albert was waiting when I taxied in and shut down. Before I even climbed out, he was waving his arms and shouting. You'd think a guy whose family had been in the country as long as his would speak American. Of all the words he spouted, the only ones I understood were *loco* and *hombre*. *Hombre* I knew from that Paul Newman movie.

The arm-waving rant went on and on, and I'd hear those two words from time to time. I figured it pretty much meant, "What kind of man are you?"

Finally, he pointed up at me in the cockpit. "You're fired."

He could speak good American when he wanted to.

I started my own duster business with three planes at first. In the fall, we dusted cotton with nasty stuff to make the leaves fall off. It was probably left over Agent Orange the agricultural supply people got cheap from military surplus. In the early-morning hours, before the wind started moving from northwest to southeast like it does every afternoon in the valley, the stuff hung in the air. The air seemed to get more viscous, like you had to chew it before you could breathe it. And it tasted raunchy. Some valley people complained it made 'em sick. Sure as hell made the leaves fall off the cotton though.

The business grew to eight planes. I lost a couple of aircraft, and the pilots too. One hit a tree. Another hit a condor. You could see how they got endangered. Too damn dumb to get out of the way of a bright yellow crop duster. Anyway, with buzzard guts covering the windscreen of his plane, the pilot didn't see the power line. In that business, you lost a few, you know?

If anyone asked that "What kind of man are you?" question about me, it was in the third person and behind my back. Being the boss was a pleasant way to live.

After four years, I partnered with a nephew of Albert Mendoza's and left the crop dusting business with him. He also managed the thousand acres of alfalfa, cotton, vegetables, and flower fields I owned.

I was right proud of those flower fields—fifty acres of 'em. I had the biggest goddamned *Giverny* garden in the universe. I'd taken a tour once during my ship's company-puke tour in the Med. I found Monet interesting. His garden was an overgrown mess. Mine was orderly, planted in neat rows, which I'd color coordinated—unlike the Impressionist had, simply scattering flower seeds by the handful over his front yard. Probably did it when he got tired of his wife ragging Frog talk on him to mow the grass.

At any rate, I missed those flowers when I moved back to where I'd grown up, which was Galveston, Texas. I can't say exactly why I decided to leave California. Flying a duster plane had begun to feel a little stale. Stale was not how a pilot should feel when he strapped a plane to his butt. Maybe I was looking for something I hadn't found yet. Maybe I'd developed a hankering to go back to my roots.

I drove my pickup into town in the middle of hurricane season. I saw blue tarps on a lot of roofs, and a week later, three Mexicans and I established a roofing business in a little town ten miles north of Galveston. One of them, Jesus, spoke American. Plenty of houses along the Gulf Coast needed new lids.

By the third year, I owned a fleet of trucks and ran six crews. Those guys were little brown working machines for sure. That year, too, I learned something. Female, minority-owned businesses had advantages. Felipe, cousin of Jesus, had a sister. Josefina was a little on the hefty side. She wasn't a looker, but she wasn't bag-over-the-head ugly either. She only spoke Spanish. Ideal for my second go at marriage.

She wanted a big wedding. Kibosh that.

"This is business. Nothing else. Get those fancy notions out of your head."

Jesus translated. Josefina's lips pressed to a line. She glared at me, spun on her heel, and stomped out.

My first marriage had lasted two months. This one might not last that long. I figured I needed to move fast. Felipe brought in a *tio* lawyer and a *primo carnal* accountant. In January 1990, we rechartered the roofing business in Josefina's name. I leveraged my California property and set up Josefina Roofing operations in Baton Rouge, Biloxi, and Ocala. We also did a Josefina Disaster Recovery, Inc., in Okmulgee, Oklahoma.

What God rips asunder, let no man try to clean up. Let Josefina.

I came up with that slogan myself.

The Lord prospered the work of our hands. Josefina Roofing developed a good reputation among insurance companies, and we did well. We made money in tornado alley and along the coast.

The next thing I knew, the second anniversary of my marriage appeared on the calendar a week away.

Josefina's Roofing proved to be the best business I ever had. Josefina turned out to be a great partner. She picked up American. I knew maybe fifteen words of Spanish. When we set up new locations, she knew what to do without having to be told. Plus, she cooked. What was that thing in the Bible about a worthy wife? I can't remember, but Josefina *worthied* the shit out of the sacrament of matrimony.

I owed her. Josefina's face lit up when I told her about celebrating our anniversary at Denny's.

We slid into the booth, and I studied the menu. I felt her eyes on me.

"Find something you really like. Whatever you want, whatever it costs."

She didn't pick up the menu. She just looked at me with moon eyes.

"I have new name for you," she said.

"Joe Bob's been my name. It suits. It's Joe Bob."

"Is Papa."

"What? How the hell …?"

"Your *impermeables*. They are not, how you say, proof of the fool."

Well, I don't remember if we ate or not. I was busy thinking. Had she messed around on me as Amanda Sue had done? We traveled together to other states. She drove a truck when we worked a contract. We were together all the time. No, she hadn't screwed me that way. I guess it could have been what she said. It was a puzzlement. I don't remember driving home. But we got there somehow.

"We go to bed now." Josefina had this glow about her. Her face was saying she had a major bellyful of happy stashed inside. "You don't need that," she said. "I am already, how you say, up knocked."

That night, I felt truly married. Of the two months with Amanda Sue, I couldn't remember much. She had been a girl and probably still was. Josefina, on the other hand, was a woman.

A couple of days later, Felipe started calling me Papa. The other guys picked up the name. Pretty soon, all of Josefina's employees called me that. If someone called me Joe Bob, I had to stop a moment to figure out he meant me.

I was going to be a papa. It felt sort of cool.

Business boomed. We expanded the operations into Florida, Mississippi, Louisiana, and Oklahoma. I stayed home more and more as Josefina bulged more and more.

One day, Felipe's wife said she wanted to hold a baby shower for Josefina.

"We'll have it our house," my *esposa* said.

The day of the event, I worked outside sanding a cradle. I'd engineered a real work of art out of cherrywood. The side spokes were close together, so our *niño/a* couldn't slip a tiny head through them, it was rigged so Mama or Papa could rock the little one through a nightmare and safely into dreamland, and it had wheels. It was a great piece of work. It just needed the finish coats.

From the open window, I heard a woman ask, "When are you due?"

Josefina said the date, and it slaughterhouse sledgehammered me.

Simple math I was quick with. She hadn't been up knocked when we went to Denny's. She had gotten that way after we'd come home.

God damn! Joe Bob did not like being screwed.

I grabbed the sides of the cradle, ripped the thing apart, got in my pickup, and drove until I came to a bar.

I used to drink but didn't anymore, beyond a beer, never more than two a night. That afternoon, though, getting drunk was the only thing on my horizon. I couldn't remember what I used to like to drink. I just pointed at bottles and had the bartender pour shots. Rum and tequila left sweet sitting on my tongue. Joe Bob did not feel sweet. Scotch left a funky taste of what seemed like dried swamp mud. Jack Daniels. American booze. A taste of Midwestern wooded hills slithered into my taste buds as the juice sluiced cold down my throat and puddled warm in my belly. Jack, be my buddy tonight.

I sat hunched forward, elbows on the bar, sipping and telling Jack what I was going to do to Josefina. What I decided to do would earn me capital punishment. It was a small price to pay. I just had to pick the right way to kill her.

A number of potential homicides skulked through my head like the Ripper through a foggy alley. I only remember the fog and that it was the shade of gray exactly halfway between black and white.

The next thing I knew, I was standing in front of St. Peter. He was up on a platform behind this little podium. He sat on a barstool. He frowned down at me and shook his head. I tried to swallow, but I was flat out of spit.

"What kind of man are you?" St. Petey's eyes had little bolts of lightning flashing in and out of them. He raised a hand with his index finger extended out of a fist. The hand lowered. He pointed ...

"No!" I screamed.

Hands grabbed my arms. They tried to push me down, in the direction in which he'd pointed.

They don't have enough goddamned angels to get Joe Bob down there.

"Papa. Papa."

The light hurt like hell. Through the slits, I saw Josefina. I felt sick.

"Last night, you puke in my car. No puke on my floor."

She held a bucket for me. My stomach tried like hell to pull itself out of my body, and it didn't care what it tore out to get away.

It took some time for the spasms to subside.

"How'd I get home?"

"Bartender. He take your cell phone. Call home."

I remembered him. E. T. Dubois his nametag had said. He'd asked me to ease up.

"Go to hell," I'd told him.

"Car keys," he'd said with his hand out.

I'd reinvited him to go away.

He was big as me and quicker by a fair amount. He got me on the floor with my arm twisted behind my back and took my keys. The rest was blank.

I stood up, waited for the world to stop spinning in wrong and crazy directions, went to the kitchen sink, and rinsed my mouth with tap water.

Josefina stood in the doorway into the kitchen, her fingers laced and hands resting on the shelf of her belly.

Nobody'd ever seen me like she had—well, except for E. T. Dubois.

"Tomorrow you build new cradle."

I nodded.

"Tomorrow you take thank-you note to Mr. Dubois."

"Yeah." Speaking hurt less than nodding.

"I fry potatoes. I fry bacon. You eat."

"Uh-uh."

"You eat. It sober you up. So you be sober when I beat you. I beat you till you be political correct. You not make little Joe Roberto redneck."

"What the hell kind of woman are you?"

"Good one. We make good baby."

The corners of her mouth tweaked up.

"After I kick your ass, maybe twenty, thirty times, you be good papa, I think."

Laughing hurt my head, but once I started, I had a hell of a time stopping.

Josephina was gone for her six-week checkup. I sat next to Joe Roberto Jr. and rocked his cradle.

The way Josephina was raising him, the boy would turn out to be a sissy. I worried about him.

As he rocked, I told the boy his papa's story. Amanda Sue was in it. A boy needs to know to be wary of wily women. After saying, "the end," I knew what I was going to do.

I'd been thinking about my pop. He was a B-17 pilot. That's all. I was his kid, but I was no part of who he was.

Joe Bob was going to be a stay-at-home papa. When Josephina returned, I'd tell her. It made sense. She ran the business. It was in her name anyway.

"Joe Roberto Jr.," I said. "Know what I'm giving you for your first birthday? It's something every boy ought to have and to have with him all the time." I stuck a finger through the cradle spokes, and Joe Roberto Jr. closed his hand around it. "I can see you're interested. It's gonna be a Buck Knife. It's used some. But you'll love it."

I took my hand off the cradle rail, and dropped both hands onto my lap, and looked down at the palms. Those hands hadn't held airplane controls for a number of years. I decided I was going to buy an airplane—a two-engine. Two engines were safer than one. Joe Roberto Jr. would be flying with me as we took Josephina around the southeast to check on her businesses.

I looked through the spokes at the boy, at my boy. He had chubby cheeks and thick black hair, and he smelled of baby powder and baby shampoo and baby lotion. For the moment, he smelled that way. Joe Roberto Jr. I thought about how we used to *acronymize* everything in the navy. He'd be JRJR or JRx2 or maybe just x2.

Then he scared the crap out of me by kind of whimpering. His face muscles twitched and settled into a tiny smile. *No sweat.* He was having a happy dream.

Pop would have liked seeing his grandson. Then something got in my eye, and I wiped the water away with the back of my hand. Then my nose was running, and I blew it in one of his Pampers.

"I'm glad you're asleep, JRJR," I told him, "cause this"—I held up the snot rag diaper—"ain't who I am."

Wimmin'

omen are different. I pretty much knew that. Until lately, I'd just never thought on it much. Until I retired, I didn't have time to think. Actually, when I was working in aerospace, thinking was frowned on. The way my foreman put it: "F—— thinking is f—— dangerous. F—— follow the f—— procedure we f—— wrote up for you f——." My foreman waged a contest with himself each day: When he gave us directions, could he build his sentences with half the words being *f* words? Most times, he came pretty close. Before I had that job, I was in the navy. Some sailors, too, had excessive fondness for the *f* word. And, in the US Navy, thinking was not only frowned upon; I'm pretty sure it was a violation of the Uniform Code of Military Justice to do so.

But wimmin'. They're like … air. Who spends a lot of time thinking about air? Of course there was the time I was in grade school and my buddy Jimmie Joe Meissenheimer and I went to the swimming pool, and he said, "I bet I can stay under water longer than you."

"Bet you can't," retorts I.

There then ensued snappy repartee. "Can." "Can't." "Can."

I firmed my jaw and stuck out my chin. "Can't."

Jimmie Joe said, "We jump in together at the count of three."

That was fine with me. I had to tilt my head back to get my chin to stick out farther. "In the deep end," he finished.

Whoa! I'd been thinking the other end of the pool where the water was chest deep on me. At the count of three we'd jump off the side and squat on the bottom. The chlorine would sting my eyes a little, but I'd have to open them to make sure Jimmie Joe stood up before I did. But the deep end?

I think of that every morning when I shave. The mirror reminds me I have a weak chin. I'm pretty sure that day at the swimming pool was where it came from. I mean, I obviously didn't see my stick-outee chin pull back when Jimmie Joe said, "Deep end." But I know it must have.

Anyway, there was no way to even suggest the shallow end at that point. We jumped in, swam to the bottom, and moved our hands like fish fins to hold us there. Jimmie Joe grinned and blew out one bubble of air. I stuck my chin out again and blew two bubbles. One bubble. Two bubbles. It got a little hard to stay down there. I really wanted to push off the bottom and get back on top, but he kept bubbling. His one. My two. Jimmie Joe's lips pursed and he blew a bubble and returned to his grinning.

Long story short, Jimmie Joe won. On the way up, I swallowed a bucketful of water and surfaced hacking and coughing. A lifeguard jumped in and grabbed me just as I barfed up the chili dog I'd had for lunch.

They closed the pool the rest of the day.

The next day, the girls were really mad, Jimmie Joe told me. The fumes from the extra chlorine were so strong it bleached out the girls' suntans even if they didn't go in the water.

It amazed me that so many girls got so mad at me over what happened. Didn't any one of them worry that I might have drowned? Compared to an even suntan, those young wimmin' didn't value a young man much. And they stayed mad. Swimming there the rest of the summer was out of the question.

Six months ago, retirement happened. I've had time to think about things since then. Recollecting Jimmie Joe's dare did that—got me to thinking.

You know how somebody will say something sort of profound, and people will nod, and there is group agreement that elemental truth has been spoken. Except when a person really thinks about it, he sees that only partial truth has been spoken. Even Dirty Harry, for instance, only told partial truth. "A man has to know his limitations." Nobody can argue with the verity in that statement. But it is only partially true. If you were to say, "A *boy* has to know his limitations," see what happens to the verity of the content? If a male doesn't learn his limitations until he becomes a man, there's a good chance his learning experience will be fatal. If a male learns his limitations as a boy, it is the stuff of survival of the species. See? At the Darwinian level, truth achieves bedrock status. But I'll confess this to you. What I learned as a boy taught me to not puke in swimming pools. It didn't help me understand wimmin'.

Take this for instance. No amount of thinking has un-puzzled for me what happens when my wife says, "Talk to me."

Talk to me—the lockjaw-ing-est phrase in any language.

Were the directive to be posed before the deed, rather than after, Homo sapiens would have *extincted* itself right after Neanderthals.

Some think Neanderthals read each other's minds. No mystery about why they're extinct.

Think to me, she'd have telepathized.

Thinking at a time when blood was rushing downstairs was not gonna happen. She waited with anticipation of thought transference. The male, mind-tied, banged his head on the wall of the cave. The female walked away disgusted. Males wound up with a headache and a sloped forehead. Mind reading—clearly not procreation positive genetics.

Thinking is okay, but life was sure simpler before I had time for it.

Life was simpler in many ways when I was working. Take shopping, for instance. I didn't have to do that, except, of course during the dog days of Christmas shopping. Now, though, I'm available to take the wife shopping, even in the middle of summer. She wanted to go to the new outlet mall. She doesn't read maps or use a GPS. She cannot drive to a place she has never been to before. But show her the way once, and she will remember how to get there for forty years.

"Yes, dear," I said with a sigh.

My sighing makes her lips press into a thin straight line. Then the line pinches together and shortens up a notch. Once, I thought she was puckering. That was a mistake.

On the way to the mall, we were cruising down the highway. I was humming an Oak Ridge Boys tune—playin' such on the radio is not allowed—when I saw this cool license plate.

I read it for her. "Artillery 155. One-five-five millimeter. That's a Howitzer Maximus, man!"

"Where?" she asked.

I pointed to the PT Cruiser in front of us.

"A R T L V R 155. Art lover. How in the world did you get *artillery* out of that?"

That's another thing.

Wimmin' ask questions that don't have answers.

Silence rode the rest of the way with us. I didn't feel like humming anymore. So I parked. She shopped. I opened iBooks.

Books hadn't always been important. I hated them in high school, mainly because I had to read them. During first semester of senior year, I flunked literature with an F minus. I started liking them after I graduated and always had a book with me. Now, with the iPhone, I carry a whole blinking library with me. I had just downloaded *Hubris: The Tragedy of War in the Twentieth Century*. Was any war as screwed up as Nam? That question started me reading about World War II and military history. I was pretty sure *Hubris* was going to prop up the notion I already had. All wars are chock-full of screwed-up-edness, but none had more than Nam. Anyway, Alistair Horne's book would wait for another day, a nonshopping day. I was halfway through *The Girl on the Train*, which is really about two girls, and it's like they are both on a train, and the two trains are on the same track roaring toward each other. The wheels are click-clacking, and the engines are chugging, "Get outta my way; get outta my way; get outta my way." If there was going to be a real train wreck at the end, I'd have kept reading. But I know that kind of book. At the end, there will be some kind of weak metaphorical wreck. Not a real one. So I read *Hondo*. For the seventeenth time. This year.

At eleven forty-five, the car door opened, and she threw one tiny little bag in the backseat—the loot from three hours of shopping.

"We can go," she said.

I started the motor, but before backing out of the spot, I turned around and looked at the weensy bag.

"I wasn't shopping for anything particular. I just wanted to check the mall out."

Nothing is worse than shopping when you have nothing to shop for. Well, worst is Christmas shopping.

We made it out of the mall lot and onto the freeway, without getting rear-ended by a kid with his ball cap on backward doing ninety in the right lane. I caught up to the flow of traffic in my lane, the center one. Ball-cap-backward guys can have the right, and OMG-texting soccer moms can have the left.

"Let's do lunch at the Bread Company," she said.

She always gets one of those girly salads with fruit and sweet dressing on it. Sugar's bad for you.

Doing lunch is not *eating* lunch. It means talking and taking what she orders home in a doggy container—which no dog, even one named Frufru, would ever eat. But it still doesn't get eaten. After residing in the fridge for a week, the container is tossed.

Seeing as how I'd taken her shopping, she owed me. I politely declined.

I needed me a Happy Meal, one of manly proportions. A triple cheeseburger. With bacon. A slice of red onion. Large fries.

I conjured the image. Now, there was a work of art I could love.

The Bread Company, I go in there with her now and then. She will never go in Randy's Roadhouse with me for a burger. So I dropped her off at home. Before she got out of the car, she skank-eyed me, and her lips were straight lined.

I didn't have to think about what that meant.

She owed me for taking her shopping, but, because I didn't *do* lunch with her, she owed me nothin'—*no more.*

It took seven minutes to drive down the hill and park and walk in. Randy was working the order window. We howdied, and I told him what I wanted.

He smirked and then hollered to the fry station, "Triple bacon cheeseburger, large fries for Art Lover."

Randy's wife Brenda was behind the cash register. She started giggling.

Over my lifetime, I'd learned how to handle humiliation. Something like Ironman's suit started snapping into place over my body till nothing could get in to hurt the rest of me. Being invulnerable a little late is not as good as being that way a little early, but it's a lot better than not being invulnerable at all.

Of course I knew what had happened. My wife knows everybody in town. She spends half her awake moments on the phone, and a goodly number of those are with Brenda. Randy's Roadhouse is a great place to take the pulse of the community. And my wife's circle of girlfriends has their fingers on the pulsing carotid of our little town. Peeling bills off my roll, I sauntered over to Brenda with my weak chin doing its darndest to appear confident.

Her face wore a lot of paint and a tinge of feral excitement. I thought she was enjoying seeing me squirm. She reminded me of the Apaches who'd been torturing Hondo in the book I was reading. No worries, not with my Ironman suit on.

"Five ninety-six, right?" I asked, though of course I knew the price. I came off my Atkins diet once a week for one of the Roadhouse triples. I peeled off an extra one. "That's for the service."

I spun around and headed for the door.

"Aren't you going to wait for your burger?" Brenda inquired.

I faced her again and shook my head.

"Well, what do you want me to do with it?"

"I want you to fix it just the way I like it. Then I want you to throw it in the trash. What I'm asking of you is extra." I peeled another bill off my roll and laid it on an empty table. "This should cover it. If you do just what I said, then you won't owe me nothing. I sure as hell don't owe you nothin' neither."

Outside, I got back in the car and drove to this little park on the bank of the Mississippi. It had a great view of rocky cliffs on the Illinois side a few miles north of Alton, Illinois. Looking at those cliffs was better for thinking than looking in the mirror.

I got out of the car and leaned against the headlight on the driver's side. Trees and brush covered much of the cliffs, but plenty of white rock showed through.

That abrupt, stony face had seen a lot over the bazillion years it'd been there. Glaciers had stripped it bare. Countless floods had paraded houses, barns, cow cadavers, and propane tanks past its impervious visage. Tornados had uprooted its trees. But the cliffs were invulnerable and, ultimately, unfazed, unchanged, untouched. I knew I couldn't have any of Stone Face's strength, but it was comforting knowing there was such a thing so close by.

I thought about what had happened. I'd taken my wife shopping. She owed me. I'd taken back what she owed me. But it hadn't made us even. Rather, it had taken us to where I owed her. Then she'd gotten even because I'd fixed things so she didn't owe me anymore. But I still owed her.

That's exactly what happened. See how it is with wimmin'?

Wimmin' have this whole nuther universe they live in. Mathematics, the laws of physics, use of tools to get a job done— whether it's cut an airplane model precisely to scale or use GPS to get somewhere you've never been before—those things just don't exist in that gender-specific universe.

When I retired 201 days ago, I wanted nothing more than to be home with my wife, to read all day if I wanted to, to mow grass and grow roses, and to work crossword and sudoku puzzles. I loved those sudoku puzzles. They were problems with one, and only one solution. And I could solve them.

The way it had played out, though, there was no place in the house I could be without being in my wife's way. When I read or did a puzzle, it offended her.

"Do something useful with your time." I'd heard that more than once. With her cattle-prodding me, I'd joined the group of retired men doing maintenance at our church. I'd go to the

Knights of Columbus hall for lunch two Wednesdays a month and the American Legion one Tuesday.

My left buttock hurt. At first I thought it was from thinking so much, but it was the frame around the headlight poking me. I walked around the car and then parked the other cheek against the front.

"Aggravate that one for a while," I said to the headlight.

I looked up at the cliff, the rich, green foliage covering much of its essence, the splotches of white rock managing to expose themselves here and there, and I said, "Talk to me." You can imagine how that turned out. I continued, "A conversation with you would be easier, Mr. Cliff, if you had some features—you know, like the Man in the Moon."

I continued to do the speaking. Mostly Neanderthal thought transferring.

I thought of my wife's grandparents, on her father's side. Her paternal grandmother was a fierce, hard woman. Her paternal grandfather was mild mannered. Never once had I heard him defend himself when she barked at him over some minor thing. I'd always thought he was a loser. She'd won all the time. He'd lost all the time. But I remembered something else about him. He was the most contented man I'd ever met. Up until that moment across the river from the Illinois cliff, I'd thought he was content because he was a masochist married to a sadist. But that wasn't right, I was pretty sure.

Nobody else walked over Paternal Grandpa. He owned a hardware store. I'd heard him with his employees. I'd heard him greet customers as if he were a king welcoming subjects to his castle. And I'd never understood how he could be so in charge in the store, and so un–in charge when Paternal Grandma was there. And he appeared to be even more content to be with Grandma than he was in his kingdom.

It appeared he was losing when you judged how he played the game from the male universe perspective. From the other universe, where nothing can be figured out by plugging factors into a formula and computing the answer, he must have been winning. It was the only way I could understand the contentment I'd observed in him.

I don't know if it was the cliff or me that figured this out, but it was a sure thing. To Paternal Grandpa-in-law, losing in the male universe was not as important as winning in the female one.

Sudden dizziness discombobulated me, and I grabbed onto the front of the car. I'm not sure what happened. The earth might have wobbled. Maybe I had stuck one foot in that other universe. Maybe I'd created a disturbance in the force.

I decided to stop thinking before I hurt myself, before I pulled a hamstring in my brain.

"Well, Mr. Cliff, we did some powerful thinking today, didn't we?"

I thought maybe he might burp a boulder or something, just to add one little thing to the conversation.

"Never mind, Stone Face," I said as I walked around to the driver's door. "I understand wimmin' now. The deal is, ever since she allowed me to marry her, I've owed my wife. No matter what I do, I can never get up to even. I can only owe her. And every day, I need to pay something against that owing—every day.

"Today, I'm going to give her flowers. Tomorrow, I will give her a gift certificate to the Bread Company, and I'll put a card with it saying, 'I'll go with you any time, any day, any week.' I'll figure out something for the next day. What do you think, Mr. Cliff? My wife's name is Melody. Will we make beautiful music together again?"

In that little park beside the Mississippi, most of the time, a big bowl of hush sits over the place. It was very much like being in a church on an afternoon all by yourself. Out of the hush, from across the river, I heard this whisper of rustling noise.

I am absolutely certain that what I heard was a rain of pebbles down the face of the cliff over there in Illinois.

"Sheesh," I said. "I asked for a boulder."

The Noble Guerilla

Emerson Sharp had a decision to make.

Not long ago, he'd decided he'd never work at farming again. But then he'd met Sally Malone when a wheel fell off her wagon. He'd helped with the wagon. She'd invited him to dinner. But first, he picked peaches with her. The next day, he'd found himself working on her farm side by side with her and her two hired men. The second day with her, his muscles hadn't protested so much. The third day, he'd begun to relish pitting his strength against Sally's hay field. The day after that, he'd moved in with her.

He appreciated her farm, especially the orchard and the smells wafting from the rows of peach, apple, plum, pear, and cherry trees. There were plenty of other kinds of aromas on a farm. He appreciated how she managed the eighty acres of corn, wheat, hay, and hemp. She hired men from the nearby town of Centerville when she needed help. Back in Indiana, on the farm he'd run away from, Paw had never asked for or hired help from anyone. Back there, the smells Emerson remembered were from horses, cows, and pigs.

Mostly, though, he appreciated Sally's front porch and sitting there next to her in the evenings.

From her porch, looking north, the lane cut through rows of fruit trees standing like soldiers in ranks. Beyond, wooded terrain rose and stretched away to a horizon muted by haze tinged with subtle orange and blue.

According to Sally, her husband, Patrick, who'd been killed at Pea Ridge the year before, said, "Work on a farm never ends. It'll suck the juice out of you if you let it. We're not going to let that happen. We're going to spend a lot of evenings on this porch just looking over the hills while the sun goes down."

"It's nice sitting here with you, Emerson," Sally told him. "I came to love the evenings with Patrick." She'd frowned then, thinking about Pea Ridge probably. "I've spent so many evenings out here alone. Having you here, it's a joyful thing." And she'd smiled and melted most of what was inside his chest so that it puddled in the pit of his stomach. *A joyful thing*, she'd said. Emerson thought that's just what it was—joyful—being with a woman like Sally.

Joy was one thing that had not had a home in Emerson's paw's soul on the farm near Terre Haute. Paw had pushed Emerson and his farm animals, and himself, to deliver every minute of work the sun, the weather, and physical endurance could deliver every day. Sunday morning, though, belonged to the Lord. But that had been Maw's doings.

Patrick Malone had seen things almighty different from how Paw looked at his farm. After hearing Sally speak her husband's thoughts, Emerson had begun to look at farming differently. It didn't have to be all stink and slave drudgery. Thirty or forty minutes on the porch with Sally made all the difference in the world. Instead of falling into bed exhausted and already dreading what tomorrow would bring, he took pride in what his tired muscles had accomplished that day, and he looked forward to the next with relish. On the porch, Emerson had come to admire Patrick Malone, almost as much as he admired the man's wife.

There was much to admire in Sally. She was three or four years older than his twenty-one he figured. A fetchin' woman, people back in Terre Haute would have said of her. Reddish-blond hair framed a face that expressed passion in different guises, like an actress changing costume for different scenes. Working next to her, scything or raking hay along with the two men she hired, he saw the determination to subdue the ten-acre field radiating from her eyes and in the set of her jaw and chin. In the evening, when he'd sit beside her on the porch, appreciating the view with her, she would relate what she saw. Her face would become a window, and he could see awe and worship as she gazed upon the green hills rising away to the end of the earth.

"The haze," she'd said, "is like a gauzy blanket the angels lay over the earth at the end of the day. It's as if the Lord were saying, 'Emerson and Sally, you did good work today. Now I will put the world to sleep. Rest well tonight.'" She saw things he couldn't—until she told him.

Then of course, there was the other passion he saw in the lamplight in the upstairs bedroom. Patrick Malone's widow was a treasure he'd found, perfect in every way he could imagine. He hadn't even known he was looking for her.

He'd been with her for six weeks.

He still appreciated her farm. And her. And the things he hadn't been able to see in the hills to the north until she'd taught him. What bothered him, though, was the notion of farming forever.

Which was why he sat on her porch now, alone in the early morning, on the rocker he thought of as his.

Paw used to say, "Early mornin', onliest time they is when a man kin think, afore the rooster wakes the first woman up."

Paw had been right about some things. Emerson had things to sort. He wanted to do two things, but he couldn't do both—not stay and leave.

There was a chill on that October morning of 1863. It was saying, "So you know what's coming, here's a sip of the ice and snow that's just around the bend."

He didn't rock. Squeaky rocking chairs woke women just as roosters did. The chill slithered through the fibers of his shirt and caressed his skin with frosty fingers—which was fine with him. He did not want to be comfortable.

The porch roof hid the greater part of the starry sky, and it hid Emerson. It hid him from Sally, but he had the feeling somebody was watching him, seeing him even in the blackest of shadow. Maybe it was Sally's husband watching him wrestle with what to do. He tipped a hat, which he wasn't wearing, to him.

He thought back to that summer day in 1860. Paw had stayed at the breakfast table, which was strange.

"Boy," Paw'd said. "Yore almost eighteen. Time you got married. After you eat, take a bath. Put on church clothes. Call on Alice Simmons. Yore engaged to her. Yore weddin's Saturday."

"Alice Simmons!" It was Tuesday, and Emerson counted. "Four goddamned days! Christ sake, Paw," he'd said, and Maw had smacked the back of his head for blaspheming.

Paw bored his eyes into Emerson. "Take a handful a Maw's flowers with yuh."

After church services on a Sunday, when the boys gathered to discuss girls and they stacked one against another, for the ones that weren't beauties, they said, "Least she's not as plain as Alice Simmons."

Emerson saw himself as the laughing stock of Terre Haute—of the entire state, he thought.

But he'd gone calling. There was no arguing with Paw. The Simmons farm adjoined theirs. Old Man Simmons had three sons, and they'd all died. A deranged vagabond had found the oldest Simmons boy working alone in a field and shot him for his shoes. The second boy had been killed by a bear with cubs. The youngest son had found his brother eviscerated and with his face ripped off. After months of nightmares every single night, the boy had hung himself. The boys' mother had died of a broken heart, folks said. Now Old Man Simmons wanted to get away from the place that had killed everything he valued. Mostly.

He did value his daughter, though he probably looked at her as a burden more than a treasure. He had to get her provided for; then he could do the only thing left living for. Go all the way west to the Pacific Ocean. When he got there, he would turn around and see if there was any gold left. That's what he wanted to do.

Simmons wanted his daughter taken care of. Paw wanted to expand his farm. And it was only neighborly to help Old Man Simmons out.

That day with Alice Simmons had been the worst day of his life—to that point.

That night, sleep would not come to him. As he tossed and turned and dreaded Saturday and dreaded supper with Old Man Simmons and Alice the next day, Candace Barlow popped into his mind.

Candace was a looker. All the boys agreed. And she'd flirted with Emerson and even told him her bedroom was on the bottom floor in the add-on room. And that she was a light sleeper.

Lying on his bed in the dark, he smiled thinking about Candace, about what the boys would say if he married her. "Lucky," they would say, drooling envy.

Then resentment rose. Paw treated him like one of his animals. He, Emerson, had not one thing to say about one thing he did in one minute of the live-long day. He threw the covers back, grabbed his clothes and boots, and snuck out of the house. He walked the saddle horse away from the house and rode bareback to the Barlow farm.

He tapped on Candace's window.

The next morning, Paw sent Emerson to tow their bull to old man Hofstedler's farm ten miles away. On his return trip, Paw intercepted him. The two Barlow boys, Candace's brothers, had come looking for him. Big Barlow was an inch taller than six-one Emerson. Tiny Barlow was four inches taller still, and both of them had big shoulders and thick arms and legs and a reputation for meanness. Paw'd given him their saddle horse, a Kentucky long rifle, and a flour sack of provisions, and told him to run. "Them Barlow boys will kill you. An' I ain't fightin' 'em after what you done."

Emerson had fled west. The Barlows had caught him halfway through Illinois and tied him up. He was going to marry Candace they told him, after which they'd kill him. "Ain't no shame in Candace bein' a widder," Big said.

Through Barlow carelessness and good luck, Emerson had gotten loose and shot Big. Tiny ran to his brother, and Emerson broke Tiny's jaw with the butt of the long rifle. Then he killed Tiny with a Bowie knife. It was the only thing to do.

Going back home was out of the question, so he continued on west. A day later, he stumbled across two men who had another tied to a tree. The bound man was a gambler. The other two were intent on getting their money back. The gambler was named Warren Westfall, and as it turned out, he hadn't cheated the two men—but only because he hadn't needed to. Emerson freed the gambler.

Warren was a couple of years younger than Paw, and he took Emerson as a partner. Emerson's job was to cover Warren during a card game. If someone caught Warren cheating or just didn't like to lose, Emerson, standing with a cocked pistol to the side—while Mr. Loser was focused on the gambler—generally defused the situation so that no one needed to be shot. The partnership worked well for more than two years. Warren taught Emerson a lot more than gambling. Appreciation for literature and the finer things of life were among the many lessons the older man imparted.

Then in a saloon in St. Joseph, Missouri, three men pulled guns on Warren. Emerson shot one, and another card player shot two of the disgruntled losers, but not before one of the losers had killed Warren. The other card player was Fred Sampson.

When Fred wasn't gambling, he rode with Quantrill's guerilla fighters. Emerson didn't have anything else to do, and he went with Fred to a rendezvous. Quantrill, Fred told him, was a man who was worth listening to. They were guerilla fighters because that was all they could do to fight for what they believed in, which was that states ought to have the right to decide important things. Important things should not be decided by remote despots a thousand miles to the east. That's the sort of thing the country had fought for during the War of Independence.

When he met Quantrill, Emerson thought Fred hadn't described the captain adequately at all. Quantrill, the captain, was tall, lean, well groomed, and as neatly attired as Warren Westfall, even when the guerillas slept in the woods. An air of quiet reserve and authority radiated from the man. He spoke with the conviction of a preacher quoting the Bible without being snooty or as edgy as Paw, who'd as soon smack you as tell you twice to do something. Emerson admired him. And when he thought about it, he couldn't recall ever admiring a man before.

But then they'd raided Lawrence, Kansas.

Emerson had ridden though the town with the gang of five hundred guerillas, all shouting and shooting. Kansas men had run along the boardwalks and looked out windows and were shot—some in the back, all of them unarmed, at least at first. Women and children were running too. Emerson shot a man in a nightshirt with bare legs. He almost shot a woman, but he stopped his finger on the trigger just in time. A dog barked at all the commotion, and he shot it. Near the end of the street, many of Quantrill's raiders dismounted and entered houses. Lots of them charged into a saloon.

Emerson looked back down the street. Bodies were strewn on the boardwalks and in the street. Dismounted guerillas had men kneeling, pistols pointed at their heads as women in nightdresses stood and wailed and begged for mercy. Gun smoke hung like acrid fog. There was nothing left to shoot at on the main street, and Emerson rode down a side street looking for more targets. He came across a rider shooting chickens in a coop, and sobriety hit him like Tiny Barlow's fist. He hadn't been drunk on whiskey. He'd been drunk on the smell of gun smoke and riding and shooting, with a license to commit mayhem in anonymity from within an invincible pack. He was disgusted with himself and rode away to the east with no destination in mind.

A lone rider would have been shot out of hand by Quantrill's guerillas; Union troops; or Red Legs, Kansans' version of Quantrill's guerillas. So he rode at night and hid and slept during the day. He crossed the Missouri River at Centerville. The loved-to-hear-himself-talk ferryman told him Centerville was smack-dab in the center of the state. "On a small map of Missourah," the man said, "if a man smashed a fat thumb over the middle of the state, Centerville would be under the thumb. Ain't no lie in the name."

The ferryman had laughed at his own joke. Emerson hadn't. With the western half of Missouri behind him, he was far enough from Lawrence that, as a lone rider, he no longer had to worry about being shot out of hand. He was in a place where people told jokes as they pulled on a rope to ferry a man and his horse across a river. He was in a place where he had time to think. What he'd done in Kansas had hovered in the back of his mind, just waiting until immediate concerns for survival diminished a bit. Now his conscience demanded he deal with the fact he'd given in to a lust to kill. There'd been no righteous cause, no moral high ground in what he'd done. He'd shot unarmed men in the back. He'd almost shot a woman, and that bothered him as much as if he'd done it. Not much had stayed his trigger finger. He'd shot the dog.

All the way across the river, the ferryman babbled on. As the eastern shore approached, it occurred to Emerson that he didn't know what or who he was. He'd been a farmer and had run away from that. He'd been a gambler until Warren Westfall had been killed. Then he'd been a guerilla fighter. He couldn't be that anymore. The ferry grounded, and the man stopped talking to lower the ramp to the muddy shore. Before he debarked, Emerson felt an urgent need to decide what he was going do with himself.

Go back to gambling, he decided. He did not want to go back to farming. Gambling was the only other thing he knew. The decision, however, brought no ease to his mind. He felt hollow, empty.

"You gittin' off?" the ferryman asked.

Emerson looked at the bewhiskered man with his wrinkled, weathered skin showing above his whiskers, which were stained over his chin with tobacco drool. Emerson mounted and clopped off the barge.

"You don't talk much, do you?" the ferryman queried.

Emerson didn't look back. He rode up the sloping bank and through Centerville. He had a destination in mind—St. Louis. The last time he and Westfall had been there, Lady Luck had smiled on them. Maybe the lady would still smile on him, and he'd prosper. If she didn't, and he didn't, well, it just didn't matter that much.

Then he met Sally.

49

A mile from Centerville, he came across a wagon with a wheel fallen off. A woman, Sally, stood on the grass next to the wheel. She glared at it as if telling the contrary thing, "Get back up there where you belong!"

He'd lifted the wagon. She'd put the wheel back on and invited him to supper. But first, he'd helped her in her orchard picking peaches. That was August.

Now it was October, and he had a decision to make.

It was dark and cold on the porch, and he needed to decide.

On the one hand, Sally was all at one time a woman, salvation, redemption, forgiveness, and a future.

There was the other hand though. It was Sally's farm. The future—it was her future. It was clear, she wanted him in it.

But it was her future.

In September, he'd enjoyed working the … her farm. But now he was remembering times when he'd been gambling and traveling and seeing some of the fine things there were in the world—things he'd never imagined could exist. He'd seen books and plays; eaten food prepared for taste, not for fuel; and enjoyed one-night women. The women had wanted his money. He'd paid it and taken what he'd wanted, and he didn't remember one of them.

In September, he'd been happy to be done with women like that, happy to be done with raking a living from other men's labor, happy to be with a woman he would never forget—no matter what happened.

Now it was October. It was dark and cold. He needed to decide.

Stay with Sally. Attach himself to her future.

Or discover those other wonders he knew were out there—waiting to show themselves to a man who was not enslaved to a farm or to a woman.

The sun, down below the edge of the world was throwing up light to wash out a semicircle of stars. It wasn't quite so dark. But it had grown even colder.

Shivers shook him. He sighed and stood, facing east.

Decide. As if he were telling the sun to decide if it were going to rise that day.

From the west, from the direction of Centerville, he heard riders coming—a large bunch.

There was only one thing it could be. Guerilla hunters. He ran toward the barn.

After the raid on Lawrence, the area around the border south of Kansas City had suffered even more than it had previously. Red Legs from Kansas raided frequently, revenging Quantrill's raid on Lawrence. Red Legs considered anyone who lived in that part of Missouri to meet the definition of guerilla. Union troops raided the same area and viewed the residents of the area as either guerillas or their supporters. Farms were burned. Men and boys were hung or shot while women watched and died some too. Then guerilla hunters, infused with new levels of outrage and indignation, came and plowed the same ground. Once the targets around the border area had been picked over, the guerilla hunters expanded their searches farther east. In late September, a reward was announced for guerillas brought in dead or alive. Rewards were paid, but no one heard of a live guerrilla making it to a sheriff's office.

Halfway to the barn, he wondered if there might be another explanation for the posse. But a number of people in Centerville knew when he'd arrived and how he'd looked with Dragoon and Remington pistols in holsters slung from his saddle horn. People talked. Especially that ferryman.

Emerson imagined him saying, "Oh yeah. Emerson Sharp. I give him a ride. Yup. Coupla' days after that ugly business in

Lawrence. Oh, yeah. He looked like a guerilla all right. Pistols hanging all over that big, black-as-the-devil horse a his'n."

At the barn, he opened the big door in the side away from the house. In the dark, he saddled his stallion, slinging the Sharps rifle scabbard and his bedroll over his shoulder to save time. He had one Remington pistol with two spare cylinders. He had his Bowie knife. No hat. No coat. No time either.

The riders thundered to a stop in front of Sally's house.

"Horse," he whispered, "stay quiet, now."

He dropped the reins to the ground, ran to the other end of the barn, and peeked through the crack in the door.

Dawn leaked gray light onto the scene. Six riders had lined themselves up along the porch. One dismounted and headed for the front door. The door jerked open, and Sally stepped out onto her porch with a double-barrel in her hands.

"Emerson Sharp, he in there?" one of the men asked. He was riding a pinto.

"No. He left," Sally said.

"Look," Pinto directed the man on the ground.

The hammers clicking sounded loud and deadly like a rattlesnake that could only speak two syllables.

She pointed the gun at Pinto.

"You don't want to die," she said. "But I'm itching to kill a man. If your partner here takes one more step toward the house, you're not going to get your wish. But I'll get mine."

Sally! The woman had sand.

"You shoot me, the boys will shoot you."

"Doesn't matter."

"Maybe they won't shoot you. That'd be worse."

"It won't be a concern of yours."

Pinto appeared to have run out of words for a moment.

"We're going to check the barn. Check around your place. We don't find him, we'll leave," Pinto said.

"Not you," Sally said. "You stay right where you are. You can have one of your men check the barn. Then all of you, ride clear of my farm."

"Rafe," Pinto said to the man on the ground.

Rafe started hustling toward the barn. Not much time to think. Best to run and get them away from Sally. He led Horse out and to the side of the east-facing door before Rafe scratched a match and lit a lantern, probably the one hanging from the nail beside the other door.

Emerson whispered to Horse as he walked beside him through the orchard. It wouldn't do to have him neigh to the hunters' mounts. At the east-west road running along the edge of her farm, he turned east for a bit and then waited to see if there was shooting or if the guerilla hunters would leave.

Pretty soon he heard the hooves clopping down the lane through Sally's fruit trees. The six riders emerged from the lane clumped together in the middle of the road. They were probably deciding what to do next. Maybe they'd try to injun up on Sally, catch her before she could bring the shotgun up.

"Talk to 'em, Horse," he said. "Talk to 'em."

Horse whinnied. The six riders all turned, looked, and stared at Emerson. No one moved for a moment.

Then Emerson wheeled Horse about and said his name and the big black charged east with the lip of the sun stabbing blinding rays right in his face.

A bullet zipped by. "Horse!" he said.

Horse dug down and pulled up everything he had. The dirt flew under his hooves, and Emerson wasn't sure those hooves actually touched the ground. It was like flying. He was hunched low over the black's neck, and he peered behind. The six were all riding after him. Good. No more rifle shots.

Pegasus popped to his mind. He smiled. The man who thought him up—or maybe it was a woman. Anyway, whomever thought up Pegasus had to have ridden a horse like Horse.

Checking behind again, he saw five of the riders had fallen behind. Pinto was coming on. Gaining even? Maybe his was one of those short race-type horses.

The sun was climbing higher. Not quite so blinding any more. He checked behind. The pinto was fading. They were passing through woods on both sides. If Pinto pulled a rifle, he would turn to the north and into the trees. But Pinto kept dropping behind. He didn't stop. He didn't pull a rifle.

Emerson didn't slow Horse until the hunters disappeared behind him. He didn't want to lose them. He just needed a little distance to work with. He didn't have a hat. He had no coat. No money. The hunters had those things though. And, too, he wanted them far away from Sally. He didn't want them to return to her with a belly full of rage and thinking it was her fault they hadn't been able to hang Emerson Sharp, the guerilla.

Behind him, the dirt road clearly showed Horse's shoe marks. Now he just needed the right place to turn off the road and into the forest. He wanted a place where he'd leave a trail the hunters couldn't miss finding. Then he'd lead them north a long way, and he'd ambush them. He'd done some fighting at night. Odds were the hunters hadn't or hadn't done much. He'd get half of them he figured. The other half would run. The first one he'd shoot was Pinto. Pinto had a hat he liked the looks of.

Emerson found his spot, a stretch of soft, sandy soil between the edge of the road and the trees and a fairly well-defined game trail. He turned onto it and made sure he'd left enough sign behind.

"That'll do, Horse," he said. "That'll do nicely."

Tree limbs and brush crowded the trail. Horse could do no more than walk.

"Horse," Emerson said. "I know winter is coming on and you had your heart set on that barn to ride out the cold weather in. But we have to drag those hunters away from Sally. It's for her we're doing this. What we're doing, it's kind of noble."

Horse lifted his tail and defecated.

"Good, Horse, marking the trail."

Sally climbed the stairs to her bedroom, walked past the pile of Emerson's clothes she'd tossed out of the room that morning after he'd risen and snuck out to the porch. She'd known he was going to leave. He'd half known it and had gone to the porch to work out the other half.

She loved him. She loved showing him how to see things the way Patrick had taught her. She had watched his love for her grow and blossom. And then with fall setting in, the bright colors of his love had dulled into burnt orange and amber.

She retrieved Patrick's picture from her cedar chest. "A woman should expect to find only one Patrick in her life," she said to the photograph of him on their wedding day. "You were a noble man, a noble human being."

Then she took Emerson's clothes and, with her scissors, cut them to shreds.

The Short, Happy Love Life of Heiny Bauer

There were ten kids in Heiny Bauer's class at Holy Martyrs Grade School. He was an inch or two taller than his classmates, except fourth-time first grader Large Louie. Louie was as tall as middle-grades teacher, Sister Paul, who was taller than everyone else in school except the eighth-grade girl named Thelma.

Heiny's mother walked him to school the first day. When the two of them rounded the church and they saw the children lining up for Mass, Heiny stopped.

"Och," his mother said. "Don't be afraid."

Heiny wasn't afraid. He just thought it was strange that Large Louie held up the round sign with a "1" on it, and all the way at the other end of the line of short students, Thelma held up the "8" sign. Standing next to the kids was short Sister Everest beside Louie. Sister Paul towered over the middle of the line, while Thelma diminished Sister Joachim at the tail end. Heiny was fascinated by the up and down of the arrangement of kids and nuns.

His mother pushed him in the back. "You go to Number One. See? Number One. Go now. I have verk to do at home."

"Bauer," Sister Everest said. "You are first alphabetically."

That was a new word for Heiny.

"You line up behind Louis."

Heiny wanted to make sure he knew what to do before he moved. Sister grabbed Heiny's arm and placed him behind Louis. Why wouldn't Sister call him Louie? That was his name. School was a confusing place, and he wasn't even in it yet.

"First graders," Sister Everest said. "Watch Louis. When he stands, you stand. When he sits, you sit. When he kneels, you kneel. And none of you will say a word—not even if someone steps on your foot. You will not even say, 'Ow.' Not. One. Word."

"Momma said if I step on someone's foot I should say excuse me," Heiny said. "That's two words."

Behind him a girl giggled. Sister got a mean look on her face, and the giggling stopped. Then sister said, "Och." And she looked up to heaven.

A moment later, she glared at Heiny. "Mister Bauer, you will not say another word until I say you can. Do you understand? If you understand, nod."

Heiny had never played that game before. He nodded.

Incident-free Mass concluded, the students filed out of church, along the sidewalk, up the concrete steps, into the school, and into their classrooms.

Diminutive Sister Everest, teacher of first and second grades, began her welcome with, "God so loved ..."

Love. Heiny'd never heard that word before. Sister repeated the phrase several times, and at each repetition, something happened to her face. Heiny watched her. She would say the phrase, and she would look up. Her face would smile and become soft. Other times, her face looked just the way his pop's and momma's faces appeared.

Pop's and Momma's faces were different in a lot of ways. Pop had short brown hair. Momma's black hair touched the top of her shoulders with the ends curled up. Potato nose on Pop. A sharp pointy one on Momma. But the look they carried around on their faces was just like the one Sister Everest's face had. Until she said, "God so loved ..." Then she smiled. Pop and Momma never smiled. Heiny'd never thought about it before, but the parents of the kids he played with in town smiled.

A smile. Heiny decided to try one. It felt kind of funny.

"Mister Bauer!" Sister Everest sounded like Momma when he ripped his pants climbing a tree. "What is funny about Jesus loving us?"

Heiny froze. He didn't know what he was supposed to say. Heiny Bauer, being at the head of the alphabetic roster of the ten children in his class, had the first seat. From there, Sister Everest's nun head was all that showed above the top of her broad desk. Behind Heiny, a girl giggled, which started a couple of the other girls giggling too.

Crack!

Sister smacked her desk with a wooden ruler. The giggling ceased.

Sister got down from her chair and walked to the edge of the step-high platform. She looked mad, but then she put that look on her face again—the smile look. "Mr. Bauer," she said, "tell us whom you love."

Whom, another new word. Heiny frantically searched for something to say.

"Whom do you love, Mr. Bauer?" Sister prompted.

"I love baseball."

Sister's smile erased itself. She looked like Momma had looked last week when he'd decided to help and had gathered eggs from the henhouse. He'd dropped one, tried to save it, and dropped the whole armful.

"Mister Bauer! A person cannot love something like baseball. A person *must* love God and His holy martyrs. A person *should* love his parents."

Sister was staring at him. He knew he had to say something, but what?

It was real quiet in the room. Heiny felt his face grow warm.

Large Louie, from his rear-of-the-room seat said, "My class never had a little heiny *on* it before."

That evening, Heiny sat at the kitchen table working on his punishments. He had to fill four sheets of paper with sentences. Two sheets were for: "Good conduct is important to learning." Everyone in the class received that punishment, even the girls. The sentence had to fit on one line. The capital letters extended from one solid line to the next solid line. Lowercase letters confined themselves between the dashed line and the solid. With his tongue out the side of his mouth, Heiny completed that task and pulled the next punishment in front of him.

Under the example Sister had written for him, he wrote: "I love my mother and my father."

Behind him, Momma was at the sink washing dishes. "What does this mean, Momma?"

She walked over, drying her hands on her apron and bent over to study his work.

"Och," she said and smacked the back of his head. "You make a mess of it. Letters go outside lines. You erase so much you tear paper. Paper *ist kostspielig*. Finish. Go to bed."

After Momma listened to his God blesses, she turned out the light and closed the door. He lay in the dark with his eyes open. It had been a bewildering day. One thing he was sure of though: He loved baseball. In fact, he so loved baseball. With that decided, he rolled onto his side and into the sleep of the angelically innocent.

Other than the first day, Heiny liked Holy Martyrs despite the nuns. Short Sister Everest, tall middle-grades Sister Paul, and sixth-through-eighth Sister Joachim all universally liked the girls and frowned at the boys. To Heiny, the nuns, in so many ways, were like Poppa and Momma, except they dressed different. "At Halloween," his friend Jimmie Joe said, "I'm going to wear a penguin costume and trick-or-treat the convent." The nuns, too, smelled of lye soap every day, not just on Saturday evening, like Momma and Pop did. But there was a sort of comfort in the familiarity of how they treated him.

Most importantly, he had baseball and football during noon recess. To Heiny, noon recess was school. Still his Ds and C minuses propelled him to second grade and moved him over a row of desks. Louie stayed where he was.

At home, as much as he wanted to help with chores, nothing went well. "Feed the rabbits," led to mass escape and empty hutches. After "Hoe in the garden," weeds stood tall and thriving amid executed vegetables.

"You wanna help?" Poppa would ask him about whatever task was at hand.

"Yeah. Yeah."

"Then don't help."

Zoe had a, "Go play," for her son.

During the summer between second and third grades, the other boys had chores to do in the mornings. After breakfast the first no-school morning, Momma said, "Go play." Jimmie Joe was the only other town boy in his class. Heiny skipped down Main Street to the other end of town, where he knocked on the Meisenheimer's back door.

"Can Jimmie Joe play?" he asked Mrs. Meisenheimer.

"No. He has chores. Come back after lunch."

"I'll wait."

"Come back after lunch."

"I'll wait."

"I am not feeding you lunch, Heiny Bauer."

"I just ate breakfast."

"What?"

"I just ate—"

"Yes. Yes." Mrs. Meisenheimer got wrinkles on her forehead. "Come back after lunch."

"I'll wait," Heiny said with an angelic smile on his face. He'd practiced the smile in the bathroom mirror until he got it just like Sister Everest's so-loved smile.

"Och!" Mrs. Meisenheimer said, and then she sent Jimmie Joe out to play.

As the summer progressed, Heiny and Jimmie Joe recruited two third-grade-going-into-fourth and a fourth-going-into-fifth playmates. "We'll wait," proved to be more effective than the *I'll* version—especially after they said it to Mrs. Fenstermacher and then went to the backyard and decided to see who could climb her arch-shaped trellis fastest. The trellis collapsed before the contest was decided.

Mothers of town boys became handy with Zoe's phrase.

With a pack assembled, Heiny led explorations along Main and Second Streets. He determined if they'd climb a drainpipe, dive the trash bin behind the furniture store, or lasso a dog. A few of their explorations caused the loss of red body fluid and pain. Then, the bleeder raced home alone, dragging a howl along behind as his playmates continued their activity.

The howling roused the old-men habitués of the bench in front of Ollie's Tavern across the street from the Bauer house. There were four of them. They all wore bib overalls and short-sleeved, denim shirts in the summer and sat on the bench drinking coffee from midmorning to noon, at which point they switched to beer. When a boy yowled, they held hands up to ears, listened intently, and scored the cries as "louder," "just as loud," or "not so loud" as the volunteer firehouse siren.

When Heiny bled, he'd run home, but wouldn't start his bellow until he'd pulled the front door open. Then he'd cut loose. Zoe would come running, and before personal conditioning overpowered her Pavlovian maternal response, she'd press the boy to her ample bosom, which caused the old men to lean forward with their mouths hanging open and Zoe to slam the door.

His steady Ds and C minuses moved Heiny into third grade. Large Louie moved too. Louie no longer received a report card. He skipped second grade and moved to the middle-grades classroom because the desks were bigger there.

Tall Sister Paul taught the middle three grades.

"Her ruler has a name," fourth-grade Ollie Fenstermacher said. "Knuckle Whapper."

Knuckle Whapper, it turned out, never measured an inch or made a straight line.

On the first day, Sister Paul called Heiny and Large Louie to the front of class.

"Hold out your hands," she instructed. "Not like that, Heiny Bauer. Palms down. Like Louie is doing."

Whap.

It hurt. But there was no blood. Heiny grimaced, and his mouth opened, showing his gritted teeth.

Whap!

The second one he hadn't seen coming and he said, "Ow."

Sister whapped Louie's knuckles. He said, "Ow," after the first whap.

"Return to your seats," Sister Paul instructed. Then she stuffed her hands up opposite sleeves of her penguin costume and, without moving her head, moved her eyes over her twenty-five students. Her lips squeezed together so they wrinkled up like a pale pink prune.

"You have all attained the age of reason," Sister Paul said. "That means sins count. No one in my classroom gets poor grades. Poor grades come from the deadly sin of slothfulness. Boys especially," she said shaking her black-and-white encased head side to side, "need physical mortification to remind them that the devil is ever ready to paint *your* souls black." And here her eyes bounced back and forth from Louie in the rear to Heiny in front of the row.

For Heiny, the best thing about third grade was that the level of play on the ball field at recess had elevated considerably above how the game had been played on the low-grades diamond. Heiny became acknowledged as a star player. He and Ollie Fenstermacher became the team captains by a general consensus no one needed to voice. He also resolved to study harder, because Knuckle Whapper always worked the hand of his pitching arm.

After class one day near the end of September, Heiny walked home with Large Louie.

"Why are you always team captain at recess?" Louie asked.

"I'm better at baseball," Heiny pointed out.

"I'm bigger," Louie said.

Louie was bigger all right. Standing next to Louie, Heiny's head barely reached his shoulder.

"It's baseball, and I'm better. Lots better."

"Being bigger's more important."

At the foot of the steps leading down from Church Hill, Heiny stopped and stared up at Large Louie. "You can't hit.

You can't catch a pop fly. You can't field a grounder. Large is all you are."

Louie pushed Heiny down. Heiny hopped back up and began swinging. His fists did not connect. Louie's did. Heiny ran home, opened the door, and bellowed.

In the last hug he received from his mother, she choked his ear-splitting screech, tears, and blood from his lip like before. He quieted, played, ate dinner, and went to bed. Poppa worked late most nights.

Heiny was sleeping soundly when the bedroom light woke him to his father looming like a giant boogeyman, like a real scary Large Louie, in the doorway.

"Come home bleedin', you vex your momma. Now you're in school, come home cryin', you vex me. Do not vex your momma, your pop neither."

The light went out. The door closed. Heiny lay in the dark with his heart beating fast and thinking about going to his mother. Before the inclination reached resolution, his pulse coasted down. Inside him, something liquid and quivery metamorphosed into Jell-O and then further into solid. He didn't need Momma.

The next day, first-time third grader Large Louie razzed him again. Heiny unleashed windmill fists, kicking, and enough growling for a three-dog fight.

Large laughed at tiny Heiny. Heiny kicked Louie on the knee. Louie howled and bent over holding his knee. Heiny pushed him, and he went over backward, after which a kick choked off his howling. Large walked funny for days. And he never again picked on Heiny.

In third grade, Heiny earned all C minuses. Large Louie had

stopped receiving grade cards during his third stab at first grade. Sister Paul started issuing them to him again. But there were nothing but Fs from top to bottom. And there was not a thing Knuckle Whapper could do about that.

On the first day of fourth grade, Sister Paul called Heiny to the front. She didn't have to say it. He held out his pitching hand.

Whap.

"This year, Heiny Bauer. You will earn at least one B."

Her eyes and pursed lips, along with his vigorous, "Ow," stabbed a punctuation mark on what she'd said. Heiny returned to his seat.

"Louie," she said with her eyes flashing tiny lightning bolts of outrage.

"Ow," he said without rising from his seat.

Sister's mouth dropped open.

The quietest quiet Heiny had ever heard filled the room. Sister Paul stood like a mouth-open statue. Jimmie Joe's mom had a book, with pictures, about Pompeii, where a volcano erupted suddenly and froze people as they were forever. Sister reminded Heiny of those pictures.

The bell in the church tower bonged once—marking a half hour. Sister closed her mouth and turned her back to the class. She stood like that for a moment. Then she turned again, walked out the door, and closed it gently behind her.

The silence persisted for a minute. A buzz of whispers began, barely audible, like when you become aware there is a mosquito in your bedroom. It quickly grew in intensity. Heiny looked around at Large Louie. Louie shrugged his shoulders. "What'd I do?" the gesture said.

The classroom door jerked open, and sixth- through eighth-grade teacher Sister Joachim strode into the room. Her arrival squashed the whispers dead.

She stepped up onto the platform and wrote assignments for each of the middle grades in each of their subjects. When she had written enough homework to keep the middle grades occupied for the rest of the year, she brushed chalk dust off her hands and turned around.

Sister roved her glare from one row of students across the room to all of them.

"Get busy on that. I'd better not hear a peep out of this room. I will be listening. There better not be any copying. Each of you better do your own work. I will check." Then she pointed a still chalky finger at Louie. "Come with me."

At recess, they found out Large Louie had graduated. He'd spent five years in first grade and one in third. And he'd graduated.

Heiny missed him. During the spring before third grade ended, Heiny had made a point of always picking Large Louie for his team at recess. On the infield, the ball went through Large's legs. In the outfield, fly balls bounced off his forehead between upraised arms. The only hits he got were when the bat flew out of his hands. Heiny's team still won seven intensely satisfying times out of ten.

In the classroom, Sister Paul was not there the next two days. Sister Joachim's assignments on the chalkboard kept them busy. Her threats kept them quiet.

Sister Paul returned on Thursday. She was a different nun than the one she'd been Monday morning. She moved Knuckle Whapper from the right side of her desk to the left, and she never picked it up again.

At recess that day, Ollie Fenstermacher said, "She's different."

"Yeah," Jimmie Joe Meisenheimer replied. "You know what she's doing?" Then he answered his own question. "She's only teaching the girls. That means I really have to pay attention. If I get poor grades, my paw will put me across his knee and spank me good. 'You want to amount to something,' Paw says, 'you got to study. And even if you don't want to amount to something, I want you to study hard.'"

With Louie graduated, and to keep his team from winning every game, Heiny was permitted to field only two outfielders and no shortstop. His team still won seven times out of ten.

Jimmie Joe completed fourth grade while earning no more than the normal amount of spankings from his paw. And Heiny, he received a B on his report card. In conduct.

Walking up Church Street to begin the fifth year of his grade school career, just before the concrete steps leading to the top of Church Hill, Heiny passed the mulberry tree in the Ohlenschlagers' yard. It was full of chippies *cheep, cheeping* excited and cheerful noise. He smiled, happy as those birds to be going back to school, and recess. He marched up the steps whistling, ball glove dangling by its strap from the bat on his shoulder.

Outside the classroom, Heiny smoothed his blond hair and checked his shirttails were tucked in, mindful of Whapper— whom, he thought, might make a comeback this year. Best to be careful. He opened the door.

"Good morn—"

Behind the desk sat … not Sister Paul. The apparition smiled! Smiled an invisible-ear-to-invisible-ear flash of glistening white. Her bottomless, magnetic blue eyes twinkled with smiles all their own. She was … was …

Heiny stood rooted, door half open, his mouth fully agape. His bat clattered on the wooden floor.

"I'm Sister Daniel," she said. "And who might you be?"

Heiny stared up at her, mute.

"He's our little heiny."

Jimmie Joe!

The middle grades burst into laughter. Heiny's face grew hot. The howls of laughter rose to crescendo. He started perspiring. Suddenly, someone grabbed his arm and spun him around.

"Mr. Bauer!" Sister Joachim hissed. "No recess. Detention after school."

"It was my fault, Sister Joachim," Sister Daniel said.

"Address me as Sister Superior. Impose order here. Mass is in fifteen minutes. These heathens are not fit to enter the house of God. He so loved us, and we must love Him appropriately."

Sister Daniel bowed her head. "Yes, Sister Superior."

Sister Superior Joachim spun on her heel.

Sister Daniels raised her head. Her bright smile reappeared and burned away the wisps of moral gloom left in the other nun's spiritual wake.

"Master Bauer, pick up the bat, please." Sister stood behind her desk. "Class, this school year we will exercise our minds, bodies, and souls. First priority is our immortal souls, as Sister Superior pointed out. Before Mass, we need hearts full of calm, love, forgiveness, and peace."

Heiny stared at the new … nun wasn't the right name. *Saint.* She was Saint Sister Daniel. Then and there, in his front seat in the fifth-grade row, he resolved to be Saint Heiny. There wasn't one of those. He was pleased about that. There wasn't a single thing about her to not be pleased about.

Having decided to be a saint, his soul was covered. While the others were at noon recess, Heiny went to work on his mind. Sister Daniel would find no reason to be disappointed in him.

After recess, the middle graders filed in, twittering like Ohlenschlager's mulberry tree full of chippies. Heiny stood up and waved his arms, trying to quiet them. But they were all excited. Sister had played softball with the girls.

"Tomorrow she's playing baseball with us," Jimmie Joe gushed.

Sister Daniel breezed in the door as the bell rang. The chatter snuffed.

That night, Heiny amazed his mother. He cleared the dinner table, without being told, without dropping a fork. After a week, she remarked that Heiny hadn't broken an egg in some time. His father said it had been a while since he'd found a baseball-sized tomato splattered on the railroad tracks behind the garden. But the September report card truly astonished—all As.

October began unseasonably warm. Baseball continued at recess, and on her every-other-day games on the boys' field, Sister Daniel captained the team opposite Heiny. The Sister vs. Heiny games split evenly. Win or lose, he was equally happy. Sister Daniel, so smart in the classroom and an All Star player on the ball diamond—Heiny knew God so loved the world because He created Saint Sister Daniel.

The Monday after Halloween, Heiny said it was time to shift to football. He figured they'd see Sister Daniel on the playground again in the spring. But at noon, there she was.

"We play tackle, Sister," Heiny pointed out.

She held up two white strips of cloth and tucked them into the sash around her waist. Pulling either of the flags constituted tackling her.

Jimmie Joe held the point of the football on the toe of his brogan. Heiny kicked off, and his team rushed down the field. He held back along with Jimmie Joe and George Grossmann, another fifth grader, as safeties.

Sister fielded the ball, started left, cut back sharply, and evaded all the defenders except Jimmie Joe. Jimmie Joe waited, hunched over, arms open. He was trying to decide which flag to grab when she stiff-armed him onto his butt.

Touchdown.

Heiny noticed Sister Superior Joachim standing on the sidewalk between the school and the rectory, hands up the opposite sleeves, a statue of rectitude. She never came out during recess. There wasn't time to wonder about it though.

The kickoff, Jimmie Joe fielding and advancing it, a pass from Jimmie Joe to Heiny, a run by George Grossman, a handoff to Heiny. Touchdown.

Prior to kicking off, Heiny's forefinger stabbed Jimmie Joe's chest. "Do not let Sister stiff-arm you again!"

Heiny kicked off to the side away from Sister, but she ran over and picked up the ball. She herded three blockers in front of her and scooted through the hole they made. With a hiked up handful of habit, black shoes flying, black-stockinged knees pumping her down the field, she headed for Jimmie Joe. Sister dropped her dress and aimed a hand at Willie's face. He slapped the straight-arm aside. Just before she sped past him, he tackled her.

He and Sister hit the ground and rolled, both swallowed by the black cloud of her habit. Silence covered the playground. From outside the stillness, Heiny heard birds chirping and the girls laugh and shout from their playground. The breeze brought a whiff of burning leaves, or of a farmer burning off a field.

Jimmie's head was tangled under Sister's habit. He struggled to get out of there. Sister began laughing. From all over the field, boys started running toward the two of them.

"Stop jerking, Jimmie Joe," Sister said. "You'll pull my dress off."

Jimmie Joe went rigid. Running boys stopped, Heiny too.

Sister pulled on the folds of her habit and got him free.

"Are you okay, Jimmie Joe?" she asked.

"I don't want to go to hell," he howled. "I'm sorry." He sobbed as if the devil already had him close to scorching heat.

"Jimmie Joe, you're not going to hell. You didn't do anything wrong."

Sister hugged him for a moment, and when she let him go, a glistening wet spot of tears and snot marked the center of her black chest right below the wimple.

"You didn't do anything wrong," Sister repeated. "Finish your game. I need to change."

Sister Superior! Heiny checked the sidewalk. *Phew*, he thought. *Not there. Thank God!*

As Saint Sister Daniel walked to the convent, Heiny moved Sam Grossman to captain the other team. Then his team went to work on Sam's.

After recess, Heiny sat at his desk, pleased. They'd won 36 to 6.

The bell rang. Normally, Sister Daniel came in before the ringing stopped. Not that day. After long moments of silence, a hum grew to a buzz, to voices, to cacophony. Still, no Sister.

Sister Superior Joachim entered, towing Sister Convent Nun. The room hushed.

Sister Convent Nun was what the boys called her. Her name was Sister Mary Francis. She reminded Heiny of a particular rabbit they'd had once. He'd left the hutch open, again, and all the bunnies had escaped—except one. It had stayed huddled in the corner farthest away from the door.

Sister Mary Francis, Sister Superior announced, was now middle-grades teacher. Sister Superior swept her hard, black eyes across the rows of desks once, hunting, again threatening. Then she departed.

Three minutes later, Sister Francis ran from the classroom sobbing.

Two minutes after that, Sister Superior was back. "You, Heiny Bauer, are expelled. Leave."

"What did you do to Saint Sister Daniel?" Heiny demanded.

She pointed at the open door. Heiny ran through it. "You're going to hell," Heiny shouted as he ran down the hallway.

Sister Everest took over supervising the three classrooms as Sister Superior Joachim pulled vocally distraught Sister Francis down the hallway and out the door, intent on getting the disturbance out of her school.

"He said I wasn't a real teacher," Sister Francis wailed.

Negotiating the long flight of steps without her subordinate tumbling down them was a challenge. "He said I wasn't a real nun if all I could do was janitor work." Sister Superior alternated attention between keeping Sister Francis moving and keeping her safe. At the bottom, Sister Francis, between sobs and snuffles, cried, "He said I could never take Saint Sister Daniel's place. He said what I did was a sin and that I was going to go to hell."

"Saint Sister Daniel!" Sister Superior hissed through clenched teeth as she unpeeled Sister Francis's fingers from the banister. "Good riddance." Sister Daniel was at the mother house by now. Mother Superior of the order would deal with her.

Dear me, Sister Joachim thought. Hopefully, Sister Daniel would not tell Mother Superior that she, Sister Joachim, had insisted on being called Sister Superior. Sister Joachim had been counseled previously to not put on airs, to avoid the deadly sin of pride. But she'd done so to try to impress upon Sister Daniel that teaching children about God's love was serious work, not to be taken lightly or frivolously—which Sister Daniel clearly did. But all that was for dealing with later.

Now she still had to deal with delicate Sister Francis. At least the little Bauer heathen had disappeared. Thank God for that. Her hands were full with a most unseemly spectacle howling and clinging to her arm.

"Walk," Sister Superior snarled.

Sister Francis moved her feet. Sister Superior guided where they went. When they passed in front of the church, Adele Kleinhammer, one of the church cleaning ladies, was shaking out a dust rag on the steps leading to the main door. Sister Superior shanghaied Adele to help get Sister Francis to the convent.

After Adele returned to the church, she related what Heiny Bauer had said to the nuns. The cleaning ladies collectively inhaled and raised hands to mouths.

A short time later, Alphonse Bauer heard the news at his job. He considered his son's behavior a matter to be dealt with after work, or better, by his wife before he got home. Zoe Bauer heard the news at the post office located in a corner of Kleinhammer's Groceries. She fled home, mortified. That afternoon, she fed a hutch of ready-to-butcher rabbits and left the door open. Then she hoed out half a row of leaf lettuce before she realized she wasn't chopping weeds.

"Och," she said and went inside, took her rosary, knelt by the bed, and prayed. She wished Saturday wasn't so far away. That was confession day. It may have been Heiny's sin, but it smeared *schwarz* over her soul too.

When Zoe was halfway through the final decade, having used the Sorrowful Mysteries as she always did, there was a loud knock on the back door, and a loud, "Zoe."

"Och," Zoe said, pushing herself up. She did not want to deal with her maiden sister Zelda Zwick. Even more, she did not want Zelda to find her on her knees with her eyes red from crying over the state of her soul. Zelda had probably come over to rub her

nose in what Heiny had done—told a nun, a nun, to go to hell!
"Och, Zelda, I'm coming. I'm coming."

Zelda sat at the kitchen table, peeled her white gloves off, and
tucked them into her purse. *Gloves she wears on a weekday.* Zelda
looked up, and as she always did, studied her older sister. It made
Zoe uncomfortable. Since she'd been in grade school, she'd heard
boys talk about the Zwick girls. "That Zoe, she is some kinda'
built," an eighth-grade boy had said. "Hard to believe Zelda is
her sister. She is some kinda' straight up and down." Another boy
responded, "Yeah, and Zelda has those eyes that see right through
you. She's creepy." *Creepy*, Zoe thought.

"Heiny. He's here, *nicht*?" Zelda asked.

Zoe began to cross her arms across her chest. As they always
did, the arms ran into her bosom. "Och," she said, exasperated
that, at age thirty-one, she still forgot her breasts, forgot she
couldn't fold her arms as other women did. Then she found Zelda's
eyes. It was as if her sister were seeing her secrets, all of them.

Eighth grade. They'd been in the grade together. Zelda was
a year younger but had been advanced, skipping seventh. Both
Zwick girls had entered the convent after completing eighth
grade. Her sister, Zoe knew, had taken up the habit because it
was the only way she had to get to high school.

Zoe herself had gone because Sister Mary Bernard, eighth-
grade teacher at Holy Martyrs, had told her her endowments
would be an occasion of sin for many boys and men and that those
male sins would duplicate themselves on her own soul. Zoe had
to become a nun to save her soul and the souls of men who were
so universally agreeable to the sin of lust.

Zoe had hated the convent. It was dark and silent as winter
all day, every day. She'd cried for a month, and Sister Superior
had sent her home. At home, Zoe did chores in the house when

required, but she preferred helping her father with the farmwork, out of doors.

When she was eighteen, her father told her she was engaged to Alphonse Bauer. That same year, Zelda left the convent and began teaching at a public school in St. Charles, ten miles east of the Zwick farm, All Holy Martyrs church, and the town of St. Ambrose.

Zelda's eyes, Zoe thought, were pawing over all that history. And they were seeing clearly what Alphonse had done to her on their wedding night, which had convinced Zoe Sister Mary Bernard had been correct in the way she'd described men and their lust.

"Sit, Zoe," Zelda said as she got up, poured two cups of coffee from the pot on the coal oil stove, and added some schnapps to both. "It's not so bad as all that."

"Not so bad? Not so bad? Heiny told a nun to go to hell. A nun he told!"

Zelda sat, sipped her coffee, and shook her head. "That's not what Heiny said. He considered Sister Daniel a saint. And she was. She certainly worked a miracle with Heiny's report card. He thought what Sister Superior did to her was the same as martyring her. He told the nuns that they *were* going to hell. Not to *go to* hell. See? Not so bad. Not nearly so bad."

Zoe's eyes blinked rapidly. "Not so bad? No. Is bad."

"You know what you need to do? You and Alphonse should have another baby."

"Zelda! How dare you? You will go to hell."

The door opened and slammed. "What's for dinner?" Heiny hollered as walked down the hallway and entered the kitchen.

"*Abendessen!* Eating you think about, after what you did? Where have you been?"

"I climbed up Ohlenschlagger's mulberry tree. I hid there, but I got hungry."

"*Menschen!*" Zoe said.

"Heiny."

"Hi, Aunt Zelda."

"How would you like to come live with me for a while? You can go to school where I teach."

"Do they play ball at recess?"

That evening, when her husband came home, Zoe told him about Zelda's offer.

"Och. Until this year, Heiny caused more work than he helped. She wants him, let her take him."

On Christmas day, after dinner at the Bauer house and as they drove back to Zelda's apartment, Heiny asked his aunt, "If God so loves us, why doesn't he let us pick our parents?"

"Och, Henrich."

"Henrich? Is that my name?"

"Yes."

"I thought all I was was a Heiny."

"God does so love us, Henrich. Do you see all the things He made happen so you could see that you are more than just a heiny?"

The car's heater hummed. The tires hummed on the cleared road. Sun glared off the snow-covered fields, making him squint.

"Aunt Zelda?"

"Yes?"

"You would have been a good nun. Just like Sister Daniel."

"Och, Heiny—"

"Henrich."

"Henrich. I am no saint as she was. Is."

Henrich looked at her as she looked back at him, beaming Sister Everest's God-so-loved smile at him.

Aunt Zoe was a nice lady.

But that Sister Everest smile—he didn't know what to make of it on her face.

Finally he decided. His aunt was right. She was not the saint Saint Sister Daniel was/is.

The Free Upgrade

My bad day was running onto forty-eight hours, and I was glummed up some, sitting in the ER waiting to be discharged. A nurse parked a wheelchair next to me. In it was a skinny kid with red pimples and scraggly chin whiskers. The kid was one-handed thumb typing like crazy on a brand new iPhone 5. His thumb flew and then stopped. A second later, the incoming message signal dinged. "Yeah, bummer," he mumbled to his phone in a squeaky, half-pubertized voice.

He had a barrel of cast material around his chest. A slat was attached to the body cast, and it ran from under his right armpit to the midforearm of his left. The left was in a cast from elbow to wrist. That slat propped the kid's arm out like maybe he was offering it to some high falutin' lady to escort her to her opry box. He also had one of those broke-foot boots.

"What happened to you?" I asked him.

His beady brown eyes scanned me top to bottom. "Skateboard," says he, and he leaned forward a bit to take in my lower left leg. My blue jeans were cut off at the knee, and it was all bandages down there from ankle to kneecap.

He looked me in the eye and cocked his head to the side, kind of like when it looks like a robin is listening for a worm. I knew what it meant. Clearly, if his thumb wasn't talking, he was a man of few words. He wanted to know what had happened to me.

If you're having a bad day, even an overlong one, if you can find someone more worser off than you are, well, it's a *cheerisome* thing. But of course, the best medicine is to be able to talk about your own problems.

So I told him.

Used to be I had a way to cope with bad days. Used to be, after a bad day, I'd come home and kick the dog. Then Marva Lee traded in her poodle Daisy for Snarf. Snarf is a pit bull. He ate two plastic dog food bowls the first week. The aluminum one is gnawed up some but still serviceable. Since Snarf began aboding with us, I'd worked real hard to avoid having a bad day. All that could lead to was clinical depression and hours of wandering a sort of Hundred Acre Wood of my mind's manufacture, wondering why A. A. Milne never made Eeyore into a country singer.

I was lucky about one thing. The day before my bad day, out of my pickup truck radio tumbled Shania Twain's, "Honey I'm Home." If I knew something about music, other than did I like it or did it suck, I could tell you it was done in two-four, three-four, or Gregorian chant—which of course, I didn't, so I couldn't.

I could tell you I liked it—a right catchy tune and just the thing to slap a hamburger-sized emotional Band-Aid on a scraped raw soul. Just thinking about the rhythm, my mind's eye was looking at red cowgirl boots, legs up to here disappearing into a black, slightly-longer-than-mini skirt. That skirt bumps side to side, swishing a bit as she sways. Next thing you know, my mind is wondering, you know, like women wonder about Scotsmen and kilts? From belly button to Eve's kumquat, the body's not overdone; it's just right. She has an angel face framed by raven hair and topped by a white cowboy hat with the sides curled up, and she's singing into this Freudian mike.

I heard that song driving home from Wednesday lunch at the American Legion, and I detoured to Target and bought the CD. The way that song perked me up, I just knew it'd be wise to add it to my bad-day emergency kit in the pickup. Prescient thinking that was.

When I got home, I *Wikipediaed* the title, and I found out one of the writers was a guy named Mutt. There you go. Writer of country songs named Mutt. No wonder I was attracted to that song as powerfully as an iron toothpick would be to an electromagnet that lifts junk Cadillacs to the crusher.

The bad day had begun peaceable enough. After I took Snarf for his morning poop-in-the-neighbor's-yard-but-it's-okay-cause-their-dog-does-our-yard-and-we-both-take-plastic-bags, Marva Lee had told me to mail a package for a grandkid's birthday.

"Yes, ma'am," said I. And I drove away and even remembered to take the package with me. At the PO, I parked, mailed aforementioned, and came back out.

Behold! Lying there on the pavement next to my pickup, a cell phone holster, and it was empty.

I wear mine on the left, so I can cross draw, like Lee Van Cleef.

I slapped leather. *Aaarrrgh!* No holster to slap. The empty lying there, it was mine! Which snapped me back to how I'd spent the day before.

I'm not a pencil-necked techno geek, but I'm up on iPhones and iPads. I had an iPhone 4—a right nice hunk of technology, which I'd mastered 7.5 percent of but with which I was pleased some. And it had this leather holster, which afforded a slick draw even in the car with a seat belt on, and it never once popped off my belt by accident. I had no intention of upgrading to the 5. Nor was I giving up my Lee Van Cleef holster. But my monthly bill had gotten up there to a "holy crap" level after two of the girls had wound up between jobs, and I'd put them on our plan. I went into this store in that mall with the big white bird on a pole and asked the guy if he could help me figure out how to reduce my monthly cell phone bill.

"What if I switch carriers and keep the same level of service?" I asked.

I gave him my phone number. His fingers did some warp-speed clicking and clacking.

"Hmmm," he said. "You have four phones on the plan, and you're only using a fourth of the data you're paying for. We can save you forty dollars a month."

"What about a different carrier?" asks I. "Could that save more?"

"Hmmm," he said. "You have an iPhone 4, right? Can I see it, please?"

Reciprocating his pleasant good manners, I punched in my security code and handed over my beloved instrument.

He techno-diddled a moment and said, "You have a 32-gig device. You're only using 1.4. You have upgrade credit. You can trade in your 4 with honking memory, and I can give you an iPhone 5 with 8 gigs for free. Plus of course we"—that *we* made us partners and equally techno savvy—"save the forty on the monthly bill."

He was smiling, and my face caught the contagious disease. But wait. "I got notes, contacts, tunes, iBooks."

"No problem. I'll transfer all that stuff over."

"Upgrade is free, and I save forty a month?"

"Cool, huh?" says he.

"A deal like this doesn't make me a Democrat, does it?"

He shook his head. "I did this same deal yesterday for two Republicans."

The possibility of becoming a Democrat worried me no small

amount, but the salesman had an honest face. I raised my hand for a knuckle bump.

Like a flash, he ripped my new phone out of a box and plugged in the charger.

"That's a different kind of charger cord."

"Comes with the phone. Free."

But the car charger and a new holster weren't free.

"The 5 phone needs a 5 holster," said he as he gave me the duh look. "With the forty in savings, those two things pay for themselves in two months." He clickety-clacked. "Loss or damage insurance?"

No way. I wasn't going to blow the savings I'd just slaved away on for hours. And I left a happy man, techno-tuned to the latest and greatest and having saved forty a month to boot. The holster sucked a bit, but you know, an ounce of cool obliterates a ton of suckiness. On the way home, I stopped at Ralph's Roadhouse, my favorite burger joint, and scarfed a double barbecue bacon burger to celebrate my free upgrade.

Which carries us to the next day when I came out of the post office and the start of my bad day. Some Communist had stolen my phone, but he'd rejected my new holster, which I thought was stupid, 'cause it had cost money and the phone hadn't.

I plugged in Shania's CD and went back to the mall. Saw the same guy, but his name wasn't Mr. Free anymore. New phone—$695. I argued about the holster.

"My old holster was slicker'n snot," I said. "This piece a crap"—I held it up for his perusal—"pops off my belt when I get out of the pickup. You should give me a new one for free."

"Dude," says he, whilst shining the duh look my way.

New holster and case so the phone stays the hell attached to my belt—forty-five dollars. Add insurance and the capability to set off a kiloton explosion in the phone, via the Cloud, if it gets stolen or lost again—forty-five dollars.

I went home and kicked Snarf, which was how I wound up in the ER—which was how, after the hospital, I wound up in an MP3 file titled "The Free Upgrade" on Facebook. That kid in the wheelchair from the ER had that file on his page. The file got 678,324 hits, which was why I seriously contemplated unfriending that dude.

That bad day just kept going and going and going.

But then I thought, *Maybe we'll get a million hits!*

I decided to wait with the unfriending and cued up Shania.

Stuff Happens

Now that I'm retired, I just sit sometimes. Sitting, with a *just* in front—there'd been no time for that kind of thing previously. Not during my twenty years in the US Navy. If my chief petty officer caught me sitting for a moment, which was majorly different from *just* sitting, he'd say, "Since you got nothing else to do, Arlo, clean the head." After which he'd go and just sit in the chief petty officer's compartment. When I did my twenty years in the aerospace industry, working in a machine shop where we cut models for wind tunnels, if my foreman caught me sitting for a moment, he'd say, "Since you got nothing to do, Arlo, sweep the metal filings off the floor." After which he'd take the coffee lounge chair I'd just vacated, and he'd just lounge.

The other thing is the six kids have moved out, several times actually. So now there is time for just sitting—as long as Loretta doesn't see me. Which means just sitting has to happen before the crack of 7:00 a.m. When she has to, Loretta gets up before then. But if her druthers drive it, it's seven. Not a minute before. Nor one after. Me, my peepers pop open at five. They've done that for so many years, they don't know how to stay shut longer. And besides, it gives me time to get my morning business done, eat breakfast, and make a pot of coffee.

Breakfast especially works better when I'm in the kitchen

alone. I eat breakfast standing up. Used to be, in the old days, when I sat at the table, I spent a lot of time running back and forth between the kitchen and the table, whereas the actual eating took maybe three and a half minutes. So eating standing behind the kitchen counter saves time and is more pleasant; I don't have to think about all the time I waste walking back and forth. The exception, of course, is those rare occasions when she rises early and/or I rise late. And we are in there together. And there is not one square inch I can occupy without being in her way. So I try mightily to never let sleeping late happen. When the weather's good, I like to just sit on the patio. Those moments on the patio are mine. They are one of the few things in the world I own.

It's like that's the only piece of life I can live the way I want. Just sitting. Our house just sits atop a hill. And from the patio, we have a good view to the north and to the east. It's floodplain near the confluence of the Mississippi and Missouri Rivers. Over the last several years, businesses have come in, put levees up, and built factories and warehouses below us. I take the coffeepot out with me and drink a couple of cups of mud while I watch people go to work at those establishments. Watching that is pleasurable.

After the sun comes up, left to my own devices, I'd do a lot more just sitting. But just sitting is offensive to chief petty officer/foreman Loretta.

"Do something useful with your time," she says.

"Sudoku puzzles are useful."

This causes her hands to move to her hips and she launches into a listing of *real* useful things I could/should/ought to be doing.

The hands on her hips are distracting. She has nice hips. The whole package is nice actually. Sleeping till seven, it's beauty sleep. It works for her.

Then I get a smack on the shoulder to recapture my attention.

And I stop considering sudoku, which I really like to work. And I stop thinking about her charms because that sure as shooting isn't going anywhere, not the way our conversation is progressing. Furthermore, she does lots of useful things every day of the week.

While I—

"I'm going to mow the grass," I say.

"You mowed it yesterday."

"We've had a wet spring. It grows fast."

At this, she shakes her head and stomps off to the bathroom to put finishing touches to what beauty sleep started.

Leisure in the evenings is sanctioned.

We, she and I, have two TV programs we watch together—*NCIS* on Tuesday and *Blue Bloods* on Friday. Last night was a Monday, and she decided we'd watch a movie together. "But not one of those blood and guts and violence things."

I invited. "You pick one out then."

She went to the unfinished part of the basement to the three bookcases filled with VHS tapes and returned with *Forrest Gump*—which we watched.

So this morning, I was on the patio slurping mud from my mug, and I thought about that bumper sticker from the movie: "Stuff Happens."

Note: I know what the bumper sticker really said, but you know too, without me having to write it. The world is a weensy bit better place with one less four-letter word stamped on paper.

So anyway, that morning I wondered, *Does* stuff *really have to happen?*

It occurred that "stuff" came in a couple of categories. One was like acts of God—tsunamis, earthquakes, lightning strikes. Lightning never struck me. I never got tsunami-ed. I was in an earthquake, not in it where damage happened, so more like on the periphery.

One Sunday, we, she and I and the two kids we had at the time, were at Mass in the chapel at Naval Air Station Lemoore, California. I don't remember which part of the service we were into, but it wasn't the homily because I was awake. Anyway, with no warning, the pew in front of us moved in one direction, while the one behind us moved in another. I thought the pews moved at least a yard and then jerked back in the other direction and snapped again to the starting position. The motion had been violent. I and everyone around me grabbed onto the pew in front to keep from falling. I worried about the roof tumbling down on us. But it stayed up there. And it was over, gone as suddenly as it came. Turns out the epicenter had been in the Sierras, some sixty miles to the east. Sixty miles from the center, and all of us puny people had been as helpless as a leaf in a gale. That got me thinking about what happened when Adam and Eve ate the apple and what happened to Sodom and Gomorrah. And, too, there was the fig tree.

Acts of God constituted heavy-duty, scary "stuff." Fortunately though, after thinking about it some more, I concluded that acts of God happened to other people. I mean, really, you see that kind of stuff on TV.

TV was where stuff happens to other people.

That morning on the patio was a couple of months ago, now, but I remember it clearly. At one point, I was looking off to the east, where the sun harbingered its arrival with a faint glow on the horizon that melted a hole in the star scape, and I thought, *I got a passel of thinkin' done on just one mug of coffee, and the sun isn't even up yet.* I poured another cup of joe and went back to work.

I decided the other category of "stuff" was mistakes. There was sin, which was a screwup of the moral kind. Mental lapses filled out the rest of that kind. Growing up, and even later, I'd made plenty of both kinds of boners.

Sins. I carted those into the confessional and received absolution. That meant my soul slate was wiped clean—like confession made sin-stuff retroactively not happen.

The mental goofs, like the time I was driving and the kids were fighting and yowling behind me, and I turned so I could holler at them, punctuated with major skank-eye, and ran into the car in front of us. The worst thing was Loretta'd been in the passenger seat.

Then I remembered the Bible had some things about mistakes. Moses whacked the water rock twice—in front of God and everybody. The biggest boner in the Holy Book, except for eating the apple of course, belongs to Abraham. He walks down that road with the Lord, and the Almighty says He's fed up with Sodom and Gomorrah. He's nuking the twin cities.

Abraham asks, "What if there are fifty good people?"

"If there are fifty, no nuke."

Then he weasels the deal down to ten. And Abe stops there! And he was doing so well with the haggling. That was a big one.

And I wondered, *How'd we find out about that mistake?* Did Abraham keep a journal? Maybe he told somebody who was a blabbermouth.

Mistakes are easy to talk about if they belong to somebody else.

I even wondered if God made a mistake or two. Take boobs on a male, for instance, the epitome of uselessness. My first navy nickname was Boar Tit. Chief Petty Officer Irons dubbed me that after I spent my first week at sea sick in bed, even though the ocean was baby-butt smooth. Male mams, useless all right. I've believed that for a long time.

Anyway, I was out of coffee, and my head buzzed like an overloaded transformer.

Enough thinking for today.

When I got back inside, she was eating her cereal with the paper propped in front of her bowl.

After a hug and kiss on the cheek, I asked, "Sleep well?"

"Yes. Did you?"

"Yeah. Good. Wha'cha doing today?"

"It's time to mow the grass," she said.

That made me dizzy. *That* was my line. I used it to avoid doing what she wanted me to do. After forty-seven years of marriage, sometimes I think I've figured out a few things. Then she says something like … *that.*

Most of the time when she wants me to do something, she worries I'll forget, so she does the verbal equivalent of sticking her directive to my brain with a nail gun. It does engender a spike of annoyance. She treats me like a child. One of these days, I'll probably develop self-esteem issues.

What's a fella' to do? I donned mow clothes, pulled the mower out of the man shed, cranked her up, mowed the uphill side, and was almost finished with the front when the car backed out of the garage. She waved before driving off to one of her volunteer activities.

Mowing the grass has been good for me. I know that because she told me so.

The front yard isn't much, but the back is honking and kind of steep.

Kind of steep.

Here's unqualified steep: Kid number two got me skiing for the first time when I was forty-six at this place near Tahoe. I'd taken the family on a vacation that winter.

When I was in the US Navy and we'd moved every two years, I'd told the kids it was a vacation. They figured out they'd never been on a real vacation. They hounded me.

So number two kid is in college, and he is friends with a

guy whose family owns a cabin near Tahoe. They use the place December through February. March may or may not have snow. We could use the place in March if we wanted. We wanted. And Tahoe had snow!

After an hour on the bunny slope with three-year-olds, number two kid took me up the mountain. I could write a couple of paragraphs about getting on and off the chairlift, but I'm trying to get to steep. We started down, and the third time I put my skis back on—oh, fourteen, maybe sixteen feet from the top of the lift—I glanced out over this cliff, which was the trail. I planted my poles and looked down between my skis. I could not believe snow could hang onto a slope like that. That was steep.

There are other paragraphs about the descent of myself, my stocking cap, gloves, goggles, skis and poles, and two false upper Bucky Beaver teeth as very individualized activities, but I'm trying to get back to mowing.

Originally, our backyard had a steep slope, but the builder had put in four stone walls. The walls sliced the yard into terraces with *kind of* steep slopes.

So I was mowing on the second terrace from the top right along the edge of the stone wall. I tooled along behind the mower, like I'd done a thousand times before. My feet were walking, the mower was mowing, and I was singing "Red, Red Wine," and feeling fine. Time to turn around. I put Neil Diamond on pause, stood on top of the wall, a five-foot drop behind me, my U-turn half flipped, when the drive wheels lost traction, and the mower started coming back on me.

I was going over backward.

Thoughts popped like a string of firecrackers.

Land on feet. No, break a hip. Kick away like Greg Louganis clearing the board for a back-twisting double octaflugeron.

Forget flugerons. Land facedown. Catch myself with my hands. Don't face-plant.

Great thoughts. Good plan. I executed.

So I'm on the ground at the base of the wall, lying on the grass, and I'm about to congratulate myself for the flawless execution of a Louganis platform dive, which scored a ten, when I remember the mower. I quick-roll to my left. The mower lands where I had been, bounces once, flips upside down, and slides to about ten feet below me.

I'm resting there, my upper body weight supported by hands and arms. I smile. A time ago, I worked with pilots who flew US Navy planes. They always said, "It's better to be lucky than good."

Heck, man, it's best to be lucky and *good!*

And immortal!

Barring incontrovertible evidence to the contrary, you can be immortal. And the way it works, when the incontrovertible evidence gets there, you're not able to see it. So you can die immortal.

Maybe you need to come close to being *Cuisinarted* by a lawn mower to appreciate the logic.

The mower is still running. What happened was, it was inconvenient to restart the mower when I let go of the dead-man handle on the mower to dump the clippings bag, so I duct-taped the dead-man handle to the mower handle.

Note to self: Remove the duct tape from the dead-man safety bar. Having to restart the mower every time you dump the clippings bag, that no longer sucks.

Anyway, I lay there and smiled some more and took stock— athletic, smart (aside from the duct tape, maybe), lucky, and good, besides the obvious charm, studly looks, immortality, and so on.

I was alive, not hurt, and holy crap—majorly and best of all and thank you, Jesus, Mary, and Joseph—She didn't see it. She, my highly significant Other, my One and Only Squeeze.

Booyah! Back quadruple twisting—which would turn Greg Louganis green with envy—*octaflugeron! Booo yah, baby!*

If She didn't see it, it didn't happen.

I pushed myself up to check on the mower, and it kind of hurt across my chest. I stretched, flexed, and rotated my arms a bit. Good to go.

The mower quit running, not having a fuel tank designed for inverted operations like a Blue Angel airplane. I turned it over and pushed that squishy little nipple under the fuel tank. It started right up, and I finished the job.

She didn't come home for lunch. I drove down the hill to Randy's Roadhouse, which features the world-famous double bacon barbecue burger. I scarfed one, along with a large order of onion rings. Life just then seemed to warrant some sort of celebration.

The afternoon and evening went okay until the end of the ten o'clock news. I pushed myself up using the arm of the sofa.

Whoa!

A sharp pain cut across my chest. I couldn't inhale. Exhaling was fine, but you can only go so far with that. It was kind of scary. Then I got a sip of air and a boatload of crap from Her after the interrogation.

She said, "Doctor."

"It'll be okay in the morning."

And then She said, "Tylenol."

"No."

"Advil."

"No."

"Aleve."

"No."

Then She gave me Her *suit-your-stupid-self* look.

Getting into bed was an adventure, but I managed. It took some time to get myself arranged so nothing hurt. By then, I was plumb tuckered. I zonked.

The next morning, my eyes popped open, zero five hundred, right on time. Nothing hurt. I felt eighteen or thirty-two years old; I couldn't decide which. It didn't matter.

Then I moved.

Two invisible, burly dudes wearing executioner masks but no shirts over their oily, sweaty skin, which was as white as the grubs that make brown circles in my green lawn, took rusty railroad spikes and simultaneously sledgehammered them through my nipples. That's what broken boobs feel like.

That first broken-boob morning is kind of fuzzy. I vaguely recall engaging in several rounds of the doctor-no, pill-no conversation.

Just before lunch, She asked, "What are you doing?"

Well, I was walking around the house with my hands cupped over my boobs. It was the only way to make them stop hurting. I tried an ace bandage around my chest. That made it worse. Holding myself made it tolerable.

I put my hands down and took a step, and it hurt.

A thought came into my head like a SWAT team flash bang skittering across the floor of the perps' flophouse hideout—*sports bra*.

She was going to that big-dove-on-a-pole mall. I needed to go to the Apple store so that I could be humiliated by an Apple idiot—they know they don't have to spend a genius on me—and there was a sports store in the same mall. They'd have sports bras.

She drove. I held myself until I had a vision of the drivers of the semis we passed on their CBs. "This is Easy Rider. Be on the lookout for a red Honda Odyssey heading south on 270.

Woomin' drivin'. Man holding himself upstairs. I'ma thinkin' those two had sex transplants. Wha'chall think, come on?" I thought about two of my heroes. Neither Dirty Harry nor the Robert Crais character, Joe Pike, would walk around the mall holding themselves. I put my hands down and sat there practicing gutting it out. Time sure went slow. But eventually, we arrived. She went Her way. I went mine.

I left Apple, blushing but with my head held high, and headed for the sports store. As soon as I saw the store name sign, I did a "to the rear, march." The US Navy had taught me how to do those in boot camp. Finally, fifty years later, a practical use for it.

No way I was buying a sports bra in a store named Dicks.

Back home, I went online from my man cave, and when I saw all the choices, I was grateful to Al Gore. Dicks would have been worse than the Apple idiot. Over the first eleven pages on this website, all the models looked to be thirteen or so, and I began to worry about the FBI Kiddie-Porn Task Force and a flash bang shaking up the man cave, so I skipped ahead to page twenty-three, where the charge would have been reduced to voyeurism of a pathetic sort, and got down to business.

Looking at the bra pictures, it wasn't clear how you get them on. Hook and eye arrangement in back? I stood in front of my computer and tried getting my arms behind me. I saw stars and the invisible executioners twisting the spikes, but I didn't say, "Ow." I didn't need Her coming in the man cave just then.

Then I thought, well, even if they come that way, they look kind of *elasticy*. I could hook it together, step in, and pull it up. I measured and I wasn't too worried about my butt. And the good news about my spare tire, it's bicycle-tire sized. The bad news is there are two of them, and the top one is bigger than the bottom. What would happen if I got the thing stuck in that big sideways wrinkle between the tires that runs through my belly button, which I'm pretty sure is still in there.

I shook my head and clicked to the next page. Behold! A sports bra with a zipper in front. Stanley, when he said, "Dr. Livingston, I presume," could not have been as delighted as I was. Forty dollars—cheap at twice the price. One click sent the zip-front to the shopping cart. Overnight delivery—thirty-five dollars. Click on that. Another click to spend plastic money, and *Booyah, baby.* One sports bra on the way.

❦

The UPS guy brought it early. I waited for him so he wouldn't ring the bell.

ZZZiiip.

Aaaaaaaaaaahhhhhhhhh!

A breakfast celebration was in order. I nuked two packages of microwave bacon and made a healthy wheat-toast sandwich.

❦

Her—I carry a boatload of fond for that woman. I think She finds me near to tolerable, time to time. Otherwise, we wouldn't have gone steady for fifty-two years.

In all our time together, we've gotten along right well. Oh, once in a while, things get a mite testy out. That's when penance happens. I've done two kinds—in bed and out of bed. You might think the out of bed would be the worst kind. Nuh-uh. With the in bed, I lie there, and the silence sits on me like the pressure at the bottom of a fifteen-foot-deep swimming pool. And I am right close to that force of nature responsible for sucking all sound out of the universe. With out of bed, also called La-Z-Boy penance, the chair is downstairs in the TV room, about as far away as I can get from "The Sounds of Silence," which Simon and the other dude sang about all wrong. I never got out-of-house penance, but I thought I did the day after the sports bra arrived.

I thought I could keep a secret from Her. I should have known better. The whole time I'd been occupied with my calling, which was to travel to exotic lands, meet interesting people of the evil sort, and service navy airplanes so they could fly off an aircraft carrier and blow them to hell, She had been raising our six kids and developing amazing powers. She'd learned how to hear, see, smell, and feel through walls and around corners. And She could read minds too, especially mine.

I got along fine with all that. Did my penance as required. But then the sports bra happened. Call me old-fashioned, but I think that when a man buys a bra for himself, it's a pretty personal thing, regardless of whether you've got a maximally significant other who will know a lot more about the equipment than you ever will. Still, it's personal.

The first bra day was good. The equipment worked better than I'd hoped, and the puppies were happy. The next morning, I noticed the box of IcyHot patches under the bathroom sink. IcyHots worked great on my back. I'd never thought of those things before I got the bra. Checking the puppies, I determined they were a hairy pair. Even if the patches helped the healing, I didn't relish pulling them off. An inside-my-head lightbulb blinked on.

She never got up before seven. I had forty-five minutes. Besides, I always heard the bathroom door. And the flush, I always heard that.

I figured it this way. The IcyHot patches, when they went on my back, started out cold, like I'd slapped a handful of Chosin Reservoir on me. After a bit, it migrated into warm. I figured I'd start with warm—save the Korean winter for after breakfast. Do a Hot Icy, you know?

I got two snack-size Ziploc baggies, filled them with tap water, stuck them in the microwave, and nuked them.

I'm standing there in the kitchen with the zipper in my brand-new sports bra down almost all the way and stuffing the first baggie in the left side when She walks in.

I hadn't heard the bathroom sounds because the microwave was humming.

She's given me a lot of different looks over the years. I never saw that one, though. Her eyes are normally light brown, a soft sort of color. But that morning, they were dark as black and hard, and there was lightning in them.

She left in a hurry. But for me, time slowed. Tock didn't seem at all anxious to chase after tick. I stood there for a moment and looked at the second baggie on the counter. I figured, what the heck, and loaded the other side, zipped up, and buttoned my pajama top, which I'd taken to wearing since getting a T-shirt on and off was way into avoidable pain. I'd just finished the last button when She blew through the kitchen, out through the laundry room, and into the garage. I heard the sound of the garage door going up, the car starting, the car backing out, the garage door coming back down, and then *the sound, of silence.*

I shook my head to get Simon and what's his name out of there. She had never gotten dressed that fast in Her life. Plus, She hadn't taken a shower. If Mount Kilauea decided to visit with a mainland eruption in our uphill neighbor's side yard, She would shower and do Her hair before we evacuated.

I knew I was in for penance, maybe even out of house.

I stood there in the kitchen for a long time trying to figure out what She would have thought when She'd walked in on me. I imagined walking in on Her wearing some of my masculine foundation garments. No help there. It wasn't even interesting enough to hold my attention.

Just going to have to ride it out, see what kind of penance happens.

I wondered if we were still going steady.

Late in the afternoon, I wondered if She was coming home.

I was in the kitchen when She returned at 9:18 p.m. She didn't look at me. She picked up the grocery list I had made up and laid on the counter—milk, barbecue sauce, pork steaks, brats, Ziplock snack-sized baggies.

Slapping the list onto the counter, She stomped into the bedroom. I heard the shower.

When the news came on, She came out dressed for bed and watched the weather on the kitchen TV while standing with her arms folded and looking stormy. After the seven-day forecast, unseasonably chilly, I followed Her into the bedroom to get my pajama bottoms, figuring on the La-Z-Boy. Maybe we'd talk about things the next day. I could ask Her to go steady with me again.

She stood on Her side of the bed and pointed to my side.

"No La-Z-Boy?"

Again, She pointed to my side, got in on Hers, and pulled the covers up. I climbed in, careful to not disturb the arrangement of the quilt. I thought a good night kiss was pushing it, so I clapped off the night-light.

The Sounds of Silence, again. It played awhile, so I wiggled things around and got them settled; let out a big breath; and told my toes, the balls of my feet, my insteps, my heels, and my ankles to go to sleep. I'd got up to my knees when the bed started shaking.

New Madrid fault? The big one!

The shaking was getting more vigorous. Then I heard Her giggle. Then She LOLed. Hope, of a suspicious sort, bubbled in my stomach, like when it's working up to a hungry grumble.

My hand kind of tippy-toed over, walking on the index and middle finger, and took a hand. She let me.

The quiet, just then, was one of those "iffy" kinds. She had giggled, but I still had the feeling this thing could go way south in a frightful hurry. She was a woman after all. And women were puzzles, way beyond black belt sudoku.

Finally, I had to make a move. "Where'd you go today?" I asked, sheepish like.

"Shopping. I think better when I'm at T.J. Maxx. I thought of the perfect gift for your seventieth birthday."

Hope geysered like Old Faithful. I thought OMG. I rolled onto my side and reached for her. My chest hurt some, but the pain couldn't compete, not then.

"Not that," she said.

"Oh."

"Sorry, Eeyore," she said.

Sorry! You're sorry?

Usually She says She has a headache, and I feel sorry. She said, "Sorry," and now I had a headache.

See how the world works? The Lord works in mysterious ways. Everybody knows that. Women work in mysterious ways. Men know that. The whole blinking world works in mysterious ways. Maybe nobody else knows that, but I do.

"So," She said, "your birthday isn't till tomorrow. But if you want it, I'll give you your gift now."

That didn't take much thinking.

"Sure."

She clapped the light back on; hopped out of bed; and pulled a flat, thin box, like a necktie might come in, out of a bag.

She handed me a Victoria's Secret box.

Do they sell neckties?

I opened it and lifted out the contents.

"A maternity bra?"

"The sports bra wasn't a bad idea." She nodded to the new equipment. "This is perfect for what you need."

I frowned. "Does Victoria's Secret sell maternity bras?"

She LOLed a long time and then looked at me and LOLed some more.

The next morning on the patio, waiting for the sun to come up and two sips into the mug of mud, I'm still sort of smiling. Over her laughing. It is the most glorious sound, hearing Her be happy. Even if it's at my expense—as long as that laughing-at business is in moderation, of course.

I swapped the hot-and-cold water baggies to the other sides.

It occurred suddenly that sometimes, when stuff happened to a man, the stuff could turn out to be "good stuff."

When you think, you make all kinds of interesting discoveries.

Kind of made me wish I'd gotten into it before I turned sixty-five.

A Writer Wannabe at the LA Book Fair

I'd wanted to be a writer since my sophomore year of college. That year, JFK was assassinated, and I married Teresa. I thought we'd like to have four kids. We had seven. Lost one. Back then, they couldn't help preemies the way they do nowadays.

We'd planned to spend four years in the navy after college. The sixties had begun with Camelot. By middecade, it had gone to hell in a handbasket. It was a hundred years after the Emancipation Proclamation, and we still had to walk around with toilet paper in our hands to clean our ears of the dirty N word flying around. Dr. King said we should get out of Nam and spend our energy on our internal problems. I partly agreed with Dr. King. We had internal problems all right, and we needed to fix them. I could not agree that we should ignore what was going on in Vietnam. Enemies foreign didn't say, "The United States has internal problems. We shouldn't try to bury them while they are sorting those things out." Lots of people said, "Hell, no, I won't go." So I said, "Well, hell, then I have to." Even after Nam, I'd stayed. Instead of four, I'd served thirty.

After I'd left the navy—and about two weeks into trying to figure out what in Sam Hill to do with myself—the squeeze and

I were both in the tiny kitchen of our rental house fixing our lunches. I kept bumping butts with her, which to me was sort of a fringe bennie of being retired from the navy. In thirty years, I don't think I'd ever had lunch at home on a weekday. The woman still, after thirty-seven years of going steady, made my heart go pitty-pat. One more butt bump, and I was going to conclude that the moment was right. She, however—

"I married you for better or for worse, not for lunch," she said, arms akimbo.

Crank up the job search. Aye aye, ma'am.

A large aerospace company, which had been bought by a bigger one, hired me. I worked for them for eleven years. I was sixty-five. They asked me if I was done working for them.

"No," I said.

They said, "Well, we're done employing you."

There I was again, as I had been when the navy put me ashore. I had time on my hands. I thought about writing, but what I did was sudoku, kakuro, KenKen, and hidato.

"You drive me crazy with those stupid number puzzles," Teresa said to me between Christmas and New Year's. "The grandkids are only here two more days."

I sighed, put up the KenKen book my oldest granddaughter had given me for Christmas, and went downstairs. Significant noise came from the unfinished part of the basement. I opened the door, and a tidal wave of decibels escaped. I beheld six grandkids around the Ping-Pong table, each with a paddle, and little, white balls flying thicker than flak over Hanoi.

They were having a great and only slightly destructive time. I slunk away to our youngest daughter's former bedroom, now the man cave, and dug out a for-emergency-purposes-only book of kakuro. Halfway into a puzzle, she found me.

Her arms took their akimbo position. "I'm going to bury you with a half-finished puzzle book and no pencil." Teresa's lips were normally downright luscious, but she had them pressed into a hard-lead pencil line. Even I knew the moment wasn't right for any *lickey* face—smooching.

The oldest grandson took my puzzle books to the recycling bin by the Catholic high school a mile from our house. I took over his paddle.

On January 2, 2008, I launched into my third career—wannabe writer. It took three years to complete my first novel. Then I began a fourth career—book pimp.

I worked my fourth career for a couple of months—sold a book every other day or so. Then sales dried up, and my family and high school classmates began refusing my calls. Damned caller ID. I found someone to talk to about my personal problem at my publisher's office. For a fee, they offered me an opportunity to promote *The Ensign Locker*—a novel set on a US Navy destroyer in 1966—at the *LA Times* book fair. Since we had family and friends in California we hadn't seen for a while and since I wanted to be a writer and could meet some real writers there, the fee was a small price to pay.

At the fair, I had two times in the publisher booth on Saturday—11:00 a.m. and 2:00 p.m. Civilians are strange in the way they keep time—and a few other ways too. But when you are running the book fair, you do time the way you want. I'm Mr. Adaptability. No biggie.

On the first day of the fair, I arrived early.

Traffic in LA being what it is, there was no such thing as arriving on time.

Once, at three in the morning, I drove into a traffic jam on the 405. At that time of the morning, I had been sure I could slither through town before everybody woke up and got in their cars.

The thing about LA, though, was that everybody who lives there, wherever they are, wants to be someplace else. So they get in their cars and go there. It happens to them when they get in bed too.

The fair opened at ten. I got off the bus at 0930—see the wannabe-writer muscle a *writerly* smile on his rugged and manly face—9:30 a.m. at the Thirty-Fourth Street entrance and wandered up the sidewalk. A lot of the fair consisted of tent booths. Four tents in from the entrance, I stopped at a booth where they were passing out free Korans. They weren't even insisting that it was the Holy Koran, the way the Bible used to be the Holy Bible. But now the Koran was holy on the nightly news. A young man handed brochures to me and began explaining them.

Suddenly, something rammed into the back of my short leg, which most of the time didn't hurt as much as the other one. I turned around, and there was a woman who looked just like Mary Lou Retton with a baby stroller. Her eyes were locked onto my olive-skinned brochure pusher, while the bumper of her stroller was locked onto my ankles.

"I'd like one of those," the Mary Lou look-alike, or maybe she was a wannabe, said.

The Koran promoter extended a brochure to her. She grimaced and shook her head. "The book, the book," she said.

"Just as soon as I finish with this gentleman," he said.

Mary Lou Wannabe didn't even look at me. I must have been invisible.

"I need it now," Wannabe said with my-ankle-is-sprained-but-

I'm-vaulting-anyway determination. "My mate's parked in the bus stop."

Mate? I wondered if she were Australian. I used to visit Australia when I was in the navy. The Aussies used to say, "We're fifteen years behind the States." They said it as if they were anxious to catch up. I could not remember seeing an Aussie in California, though. Maybe they didn't want to catch up to that part of us.

When I stood up from rubbing the back of my leg, Mary Lou Wannabe was moving purposely toward Thirty-Fourth Street, and people were moving out of her way. I guessed they knew they were invisible too.

A Koran and eleven brochures in hand, I cased the place pretty thoroughly and found an Ayn Rand booth. It was one of only two single-author booths I found under tents outside. The other booth belonged to a medical doctor who had written a number of books, but I'd never heard of him. I wondered whether he was a writer. Did people have to know you were a writer for you to be one? Clearly this doctor had to be a notch above a wannabe such as myself, given my one, humble self-published effort. I was pondering those questions when I came to Ms. Rand's booth.

Manning the booth was a skinny woman, dark hair pulled back in a ponytail that wouldn't tolerate a wild hair escaping to do its own thing. She munched on a stalk of celery and looked like she could use some cheering up.

"Would you sign a copy of *Fountainhead*, please, Ayn?" I asked, and I even pronounced it correctly. According to Wikipedia, which I had Googled on my iPhone, it's pronounced like *ain't* without the T.

That pale, skinny young woman blistered my ears with words I hadn't heard since my boot camp chief petty officer had invited me to clean the barracks, "Properly this f——ing time!" "Making fun of the sacred memory of Mz. Rand," was the only part fit to mention in mixed readership. My midwestern attempt at book-fair humor hadn't worked in California, so I offered her a Reese's Peanut Butter Cup.

Hard, black eyes lasered me. Then her chiseled, angry face softened, and her eyes drifted above me. I was pretty sure I knew what was going on. My wife had taken me to her yoga class a couple of times. The girl had major "Ah ooooms" going on.

And me, I was rendered invisible by about the second "Ah oom."

I stood there just looking at Ayn Rand's booth-*meisteress*. Being invisible, I didn't think I would bother anyone. It seemed to me that, if you were a writer, it didn't really matter if you were dead or alive, except of course for the problem with tenses. In my high school lit classes, all the books we'd had to read were by writers who were already dead.

For a wannabe, though, it was important to be alive.

Ayn Rand was giving me a headache, and it was time to hustle over to my publisher's booth to pass out complimentary copies of my book. After an hour of that, I went back to the hotel to collect my wife.

She never has been a morning person, which was one reason I had to go back to collect her. The other reason was that she was like an admiral. She knew the tactical and strategic value of sending expendable PT boats and destroyers out in front of the high-value ships. In addition to gathering free books, passing out free books, and insulting dead writers, I had been scouting for the admiral.

On the return trip to the fair, we were lucky. A hotel shuttle van was leaving, and there were seats available. My wife and I got the middle bench seat. A man and woman, late thirties, early forties maybe, occupied the front seat. They didn't look Californian, so I trusted my age estimate. There was something about the man. I just knew he was not a wannabe. He didn't look around when we got in, so I didn't say anything.

"Are you on a panel?" came from the seat behind us.

A young woman was sitting there—trim; nice-looking; wearing a functional, tasteful, understated elegance black pantsuit. She looked a lot like Mary Lou Retton.

I explained to Mary Lou Two that I had self-published a book and was passing out promotional copies. Then it happened again. I became simultaneously invisible and annoyingly in the way. The guy in front was a poet, and he had been a runner up in the book festival poetry contest. He was on his way to be a panelist. Mary Lou Two wrote works in the YA, or young adult, genre. She was on her way to be a panelist too. And they clearly wanted to talk to each other and not to me or the Squeeze.

My jaws began to grind my molars together. I don't mind being an asocial misfit, but I liked it to happen on my terms, not being shoved into the role. The Squeeze picks up on these things. She patted my hand.

The van dumped us out after a long, time-wise, ride, and the panelists strode purposefully on their way. The Squeeze said, "Here's what happened." Because of my advanced social ineptitude, she felt obligated to explain things to me. "She saw your sport coat and thought you were a panelist."

I had worn a sport coat, no tie, in the morning. Pretty quickly, it was clear I was overdressed. When I had gone back for her, my wife had been waiting for me in the lobby, and I hadn't wanted to bother with going up to dump the jacket in the room.

"When you answered her question," she continued, "you exposed yourself to her as a wannabe. She and the poet have established themselves enough to be panelists here. Within the context of this book fair, those two have extra status. For the two days of the fair, they are more than they were before or are after."

"So it's like at the low end of the scale is the wannabes," I said. "At the high end of the scale are the *BE*s. They BE Somebody. Clearly a case for capital B, capital E. In the middle are the *be*s— little b, little e. They be somebody, and they be somebody sort of extra here at the fair. Wannabes, bes, and BEs. Like that?"

She frowned and then shook her head. "It's like being a newbie," my Squeeze said. "The whole time you were in the navy, you said you never stopped being a newbie. 'Finally get a handle on a job. Then they move you, and you are a newbie again.' Did I quote you accurately?"

I shrugged.

"You said the same thing about your industry jobs. You never stop being a newbie. You want to be a writer, you have to be a newbie, at least for a while."

"No," I said. "This is different. In the navy, they said a newbie didn't *know* squat. Those *BE*s, they said I *wasn't* squat. That's different."

The wife kissed me on the cheek and smiled sweetly.

"Buck up, little camper"—a line from the movie *Better Off Dead*, a favorite of the girls and me. "We'll get through this together."

Then she shook her head, again, and walked off to the session she wanted to attend. The woman who had played Nellie Olsen on *Little House on the Prairie* was giving a presentation—Nellie Olsen, the most hated girl in America. I wondered if she ever wanted to be invisible.

After my afternoon time in the booth, the publisher's booth-*meister* offered me time the next afternoon. Someone had cancelled. I still had books to give away, so I said, "Sure."

That night on the hard hotel bed—my sleep number is minus twenty—Teresa slipped quickly into the sleep of the 100 percent innocent and justified. I lay there bothered by the notion of being invisible and in the way at the same time. It seemed like a violation of a law of physics or something. The headache came pretty quickly.

I started my prayers with a, "Thank you, God, for Teresa. A fine hunk of woman, she is." And I thanked him for the BEs, the bes, and the wannabes who filled the writing world with good stuff. I tried to make sure He didn't think the wannabe prayer was for me, personally. Nellie Olsen's portrayer could use a little attention I told him—even though the most hated girl in America made money, whereas for us wannabes, our pay was lower than my sleep number. "But, please, God, despite Mary Lou the first, and Mary Lou the second, please let Mary Lou the nothing—the real one—know that I admire her."

The second day, Sunday, dawned. We had fresh smog to breathe. It was a bright new day, and it was good to be alive. Sleep is overrated. I used to say it myself. Did me a fair amount of good, though.

Back at the fair and halfway through my last session signing and giving away copies of my book, a woman came up and asked me if she could have a copy.

The woman was about five foot nine, so I didn't have to look up to her too much. She asked me how long it had taken me to write the book. I told her and told her how many times I'd thought I was finished only to find inescapable evidence that it needed to be made better. She said she was working on a memoir of her time as a nurse on medevac flights out of Vietnam in the late sixties and early seventies.

"I've run into a roadblock," she said.

I was sure she hadn't used "writer's block" on purpose. I liked her for that. I told her I'd been to a Missouri Writers' Guild conference and that the theme had been "Just Write." I said I thought that had been good advice for me, and it might be for her too. Flash fiction and poetry contests—those were two things I'd recently done. And I felt the exercises had helped me tremendously in pushing my craft or art or whatever it was forward.

"Don't you quit," I said. "Your story sounds interesting as all get-out to me. Just keep writing."

The gray, bobbed-haired former medevac nurse just stood there looking at the back of my little tent for a long moment. I thought she was seeing a C-41 with litters three high along each side bearing wounded, burned, and maimed. I thought she was seeing that those boys were not going home. They were going to a future where the realm of things they could want to be had been incomprehensibly shattered.

I could see her with them.

She cleared her throat, smiled, and told me she had come by bus from Long Beach. Construction had messed up the routes she normally took. She had gotten frustrated and almost turned around. But she was glad she'd come. "You made my day," she said. "You made the trip worthwhile."

I was trying to think of how to tell the medevac nurse how much talking with her had meant to me when she held my book up, nodded thanks, and started walking toward the Thirty-Fourth Street bus stop.

The sidewalk curved, and I lost sight of her.

That night, Teresa wanted to hit a sushi bar.

"Sure." It'd knock a decade off my purgatory time.

She got some kind of salmon rolls. I took a vegan plate. We found a booth, slid in, and said our prayer. She took a dainty nip of her dinner. She took some time while her taste buds worked that stuff over like a CSI team. "Not bad," she said and bit off half the roll.

I was pouring bacon bits from a baggie onto my stuff when she interrupted me.

"You didn't get to meet any writers."

"I was planning on going to a session today, but that extra booth time came up. I'm glad I took it. I met a woman. Did more for me than meeting a real writer would have."

She looked at me with her left brow independently elevated. "A woman?"

"Um, uh. Well. Yeah. She was a woman, but she was old."

"How old?"

"Well. Old. Like we are."

"Old. Like me?"

"Wait!"

She giggled. It was so easy to get me going down side bunny trails.

"What I meant was she was a nurse. During Nam, she tended wounded soldiers on medevac flights from Saigon to the States. She wanted to write about it, but she has, you know, writer's block. She said talking to me was going to get her story moving again. Made me proud to be a wannabe. You know?"

She leaned across the table and placed her hand atop mine.

She batted eyelids at me.

"I am so proud to be married to the most wonderful wannabe in the whole wide world."

My face got hot. Under my sport coat, it got hot, and I shucked it.

After my face temperature got back down to about 120— Celsius—Mr. Romantic made his move.

"Bacon bits for your sushi? I'll share."

The Past Is Neat; the Present Sucks

Instead of a man cave, I have the Write Place.

It holds my writing stuff—dictionaries, American, British, and other foreign language ones; grammar books; thesauri; and a Bible and a Koran. Military memorabilia hang on the walls. An Eeyore doll, which my oldest daughter gave me for some reason or another, sits on a shelf.

A man cave is sacred, inviolable even. But a Write Place isn't even respected. When the five daughters visit, they march in and click refrigerator magnets on my big whiteboard, which I use to plot stories.

One magnet says, "Men have feelings too. Sometimes we feel hungry." Another shows a picture of a five-year-old girl holding the reins to a besaddled Great Dane, and she says, "Hey, this ain't no stinkin' pony"—which, I suppose, is some kind of editorial comment on the kind of father I've been. And then there's "Animals are neat. People suck."

Occasionally, something gets me to thinking. That last one kicked something loose upstairs, and I realized I really didn't have a philosophy like the "people suck" one.

The world was going to hell in a handbasket and it was

hell-bent for leather to get there. Well, that wasn't a philosophy. It was a statement of a conclusion based on observation conducted through scientific methodology, which, before I had the Write Place, was to sit on the back patio with a mug of mud and watch the world go by and register what I saw.

Every morning, my beady little orbs of observation beheld the same thing. Who needs to watch the world go by, who needed to read the paper or watch TV to know where the world was headed?

As for TV, I did watch *NCIS*. At least there, bad guys were brought to justice once a week—except when the producers ran a two-parter.

A couple of months ago, I was in the Write Place, and I was thinking. It was giving me a headache. I considered taking a baby aspirin, but my eyes settled on the "Animals are neat" magnet. *Self,* I asked myself, *how about, "The Past is Neat; the Present Sucks"?*

Whoa!

Now there was a philosophy.

And since I was busy thinking, I thought about God. In His God cave. Looking down on us modern humans. And I heard Him say, "This indeed is a stiff-necked people. They saw what happened when they ate the apple. They saw what happened to Sodom and Gomorrah. Yet, they persist stubbornly in their nastiness."

Whoa! God agreed with me—you know, that the past, even if it wasn't all the way to neat, was at least better than what's going on today.

What a fine morning. I had a philosophy to live by, and God agreed with it.

The phone rang.

It was never for me.

"It's for you," she hollered from the kitchen.

"Who is it?"

"Pick up the dad-burned phone!"

"No need to get huffy about it," I mumbled, figuring she wouldn't hear with the water running in the sink.

"I heard that."

Oops!

So I picked up and said, "Lo."

"It's Fred," a voice said.

I irradiated the phone with radioactive silence.

"From church."

I wondered how long he'd stay with me if I didn't say anything.

"I can hear you breathing. If you hang up, I'll come over to your house. Your wife will let me in."

Rats! "What?"

"I'm calling to invite you on a retreat with twenty of us from the parish."

"Retreat?" I stuck out my chin like the ram on a trireme. "I don't retreat!"

"Look," Fred said. "It's a time to move away from the world for a couple of days—to renew or to establish for the first time a closer relationship with God."

"So you're saying I'm a heathen and need to find Jesus?"

"Of course not. I see you in church. I was reluctant to go on a retreat the first time, but I went. The Jesuit retreat leader always gives me something to think about. The way I look at it, I've had Jesus in my heart since baptism. But I need a little help now and then to keep Him in my mind. Retreat helps me do that. I've gone thirty-seven years in a row. I get a lot out of them every year. I think you would too."

That stumped me.

Since I didn't speak, he did. "I go on retreat to—" (Fred is in the choir. He does solos. He's good.) He sang: "To see the Lord more clearly / Love Him more dearly / Follow Him more nearly."

Dad-burned Fred! Not much gets to me. Music does though, especially when something really good sneaks up on me and makes my Adam's apple cantaloupe-size. Dad-burned Fred sings like Plácido Domingo.

"Day by day," I croaked. Singing is supposed to be twice praying. My singing is about one-eleventh of praying.

⚒

The night we got to the Whitehouse Center, the Jesuit retreat leader explained the silence business.

"We can't talk to each other?" I piped from the last pew in the chapel.

He smiled and then nodded.

Stupid Fred. If he'd have told me that from the git-go, I'd have signed up right away. What better reason was there to go to someplace with seventy-eight other people than they can't talk to you and you can't talk to them? My kinda place.

The first morning, I woke at 0445. I generally do. They told us the night before that reveille was at 0700. 0700! Really? Who the Sam Hill sleeps that late?

Anyway, at 0445, I got dressed and went down for a cup of joe. My intention was to watch the sunrise, the whole thing, from total black to the entire great ball of fire—which phrase always evoked an image of Jerry Lee Lewis banging on a piano and openmouthed howling the words so you could see his uvula vibrating like crazy—above the horizon. Before, I had only watched snippets of the rise. A guy has things to do, you know—places to go, people to avoid meeting. But on retreat, between five and seven, what else was I going to do?

With a cup of coffee in hand, I'd intended watching it.

"Poop." The pot was cold. Serving wenches had it easy at that place.

The center sat on wooded acres south of St. Louis on a bluff overlooking the Mississippi. Across the river lay floodplain farmland stretching a couple of miles to a treed ridge. Above that ridge, that was where the sun would rise. The night before, I'd picked an observation spot away from the dorms, in the trees, and with a bench to sit on. I thought I'd be alone there.

A bazillion mosquitoes awaited me. I didn't have coffee, but they had breakfast. Crickets. Two bazillion cricking away. Cicadas. A bullfrog. Some kind of bird mourning a lost worm or something. I wished I'd gone to a Franciscan retreat house. The order of St. Francis would get the local animal life to observe silence too.

Ahhh! Above the ridge in Illinois, a diminution of dark. A herald.

Gack. Whack. Hack.

Eeeeuw! Off to my right, a cigarette smoker. He hacked up a loogie that had to weigh a quarter pound.

"Ssshhh," I whispered.

The mosquitoes, crickets, and cicadas—they all shut up. Not that guy. He hacked up another.

Above the ridge, a bit of red had tinged a swath of sky above the black ridge. It was as if Van Gogh had painted the horizon with a streak of ear blood. The mosquitoes were gone. They must have heard the smoker and gone after him. Mosquitoes, I'd heard, didn't bother heavy smokers. But a lot of stuff you hear as gospel turns out to be heresy. Maybe mosquitoes considered smokers' blood to be like barbecue or something. Whatever. The ornery little vampires were gone.

Now, a lot more red smeared the sky.

Woo woo!

Dear Lord! A train. Across the river. Across the floodplain farms and up against the Illinois ridgeline, the Cyclops light danced up and down.

Woooo. Woo woo.

How did that line go? Hear that lonesome whistle wail? Something like that. What I wanted to be was lonesome. What I wanted to be was alone—totally, completely all alone. Solitary. And I wanted it to be silent.

Then I noticed it was silent—no bugs, no birds, no loogie launchers. Even the train had shut up.

I looked to the east just as one laser beam of retina-frying white light blazed over the ridge and stabbed my left eyeball.

"Oh, Jesus," I said, holding a hand over my eye.

Why are you fighting Me?

That scared the crap out of me. It was like a voice but not one my ears heard. My feet started pushing backward, but the steel frame of the bench I sat on was bolted to concrete.

You can't run away.

It was such a gentle voice. It poured calm over and into me.

Something pulled my eyes back to the sun. It hurt. I couldn't look away. I couldn't even raise my hand to shield my eyes.

As suddenly as it had come, the beam vanished. But the fire of it still burned in my vision. I couldn't see my hands—well, not clearly, with peripheral vision, a little.

I wondered if I'd damaged my eyes permanently.

I closed them and still saw the fire.

I wondered if I'd heard God speak to me.

Why are you fighting Me? If He didn't say that, who did?

My vision was still blurry, but I thought it might be clearing up. The sun was throwing more light on the world. I made out trees. The river down below came into focus.

It was definitely coming back.

Good.

I did not want to try to explain how I'd been blinded: "You see, it's this way. There is a man in the moon, but God is in the sun. I saw him this morning when He came up. He spoke to me."

"He spoke to you?"

"Yes, sir."

"And you looked at him and that's what affected your vision?"

A few minutes later, the eyes worked fine. I didn't have anything to explain. The morning and afternoon went fine. In the evening, we had Mass. And we sang. And the singing was good, even though I sang too. It being a men's retreat, we sang in a manly key. Everything went fine until we sang "The Servant Song." It has these two lines that ask, "Would you kiss a leper clean?" We sang that, and I couldn't sing the second one, "And do such things unseen?" I had a grapefruit stuck in my throat.

I sat in my pew thinking about kissing a leper—all the way to clean.

I thought about that morning waiting for the sun and hearing the smoker cough.

I thought about God asking me why I was fighting Him.

And I tried to figure out how those three things tied together. It was beyond me.

That night, I did my, "Now I lay me."

Then I said, "So. God, you are taking care of the other half of the world while we sleep here. That it?"

He didn't answer me.

Maybe He is in the sun. I'll ask Him tomorrow. If He comes back.

Then I slept the sleep of the innocent, the justified, the oblivious.

The next morning, I was out there again. I took sunglasses. I almost broke my leg walking to my bench. Then I took the sunglasses off till later.

The smoker was out there too—hacking up chunks of lung.

I knew what I was supposed to do. I didn't want to. I really didn't want to. But I headed for him. He wheezed and hacked now and then, so I could stay on course. When I found him, he was sitting on one of those walkers with a seat to it.

The light wasn't good. I couldn't see his face.

"What the hell you want?" he snapped.

I bent over and hugged him.

"Get the hell away from me, you queer."

I ran.

Back to my room.

I stripped off my clothes, showered, and put on yesterday's. Then I hustled back out to my spot. I made it before He came up. I sat on the bench and put on the sunglasses.

It got a little lighter—in the east, where that was supposed to happen. Bugs and birds sang. The train over in Illinois *woo woo*-ed. *Haaaak. Ptooey.*

The gang's all here.

He came up.

"How'd I do?" I whispered.

He laughed.

"Wasn't that what You wanted me to do? Wait. Are you saying I didn't have to hug that … man?"

God LOL-ed.

I listened to Him laugh.

Then I asked, "Are You really in the sun?"

"If that's where you look for Me."

Later, that afternoon, when it was time to leave, I met Fred in the parking lot to ride home with him. I looked at him, and the tears started; snot started. Heck. I probably hacked up a loogie. Fred dug a handful of Kleenexes—tissues they call it now, I guess—from a pocket. He handed it to me.

"I told you," he said.

Usually, I prefer to be right and other people wrong. That afternoon, though, with my handful of tissues soggy with various bodily fluids, it didn't matter a whit who was right and who was wrong.

What mattered was that that afternoon, the present was neat, as neat as anything I'd experienced in the past.

I offered the tissues back to Fred.

He rolled his eyes and headed for the car.

The Face in the Mirror

She astounded Willie Walters.

"Go ahead. Hit me!"

Where the Sam Hill had that come from? He and Marla had been married forty-two years. Never once in that span of time had he considered slapping her. Punching with a closed fist wasn't even imaginable.

"Hit you?" Willie asked. He stayed put, leaning against the kitchen counter.

She stood arms akimbo in the doorway to the hall glaring at him.

"I'd never hit you. Why would you even think that?"

"Your face!" She snatched her coat from the closet.

My face?

Before he could figure out what might be wrong with his face, she zipped up and snapped, "I'm going to Irma's."

Irma. High school classmate to Willie and Marla, Irma had outlived one husband and divorced two others. When Marla and Irma got together, they talked as if words gushed out of the world through a huge, gaping hole, and if the two of them didn't talk fast, all the words would be gone before they could disclose vital and treasured information.

Things, he thought, *sure can change in a big way in a little bit of time.*

Marla, when she wanted to, hustled.

Sounds—the mudroom door slammed, the garage door rose, the car started and backed out, the garage door descended. Silence. Profound silence, as if not only words, but all sound had evaporated. Or maybe there was sound but only in the woods where trees fell with no one around.

That was funny, he thought.

Yeah, funny, in a sad, pathetic, maudlin, morose, depressing, maggots-eating-your-belly-away-from-the-inside sort of way.

What the hell had happened this morning? What the hell had started this argument? Lately, their disagreements didn't escalate in a gradual fashion. From dormancy, they step-functioned into full-blown fury that filled his head with white-hot anger. But he'd never once thought of hitting her. Where had that come from?

After topping off his mug, he tried to reconstruct the critical moments of the blowup.

He'd been standing in the kitchen, and he'd been feeling fine. Then she'd surprised him by coming into the kitchen forty minutes ahead of her usual time. She'd said something. It had been snarky. It must have been, though he couldn't remember what she'd said.

The first thing he remembered saying was "Why'd you get mad at me?"

"*You* got mad at *me!*"

"You got mad first. I was just defending myself."

It was like the anger flared up so hot it burned away short-term memory, for both of them. They could never agree on how those first critical seconds had transpired.

The thought that it really might have been all his fault niggled at him, as it always did. But he applied his engineer and manager mind to the problem and found not one shred of evidence he'd provoked the exchange.

Still, that critical moment of blowup eluded him.

The morning had started like mornings always did—well, almost.

Three hundred sixty-four days a year, he woke between five and five fifteen, finished breakfast, and was at his computer in the man cave well before she awoke at seven. That morning, however, he'd slept in till five forty-four. At six twenty, he'd been leaning against the granite countertop by the sink, munching toast, savoring the aroma of his Italian roast coffee, and admiring their remodeled kitchen. And savoring the memory of working the remodeling project with Marla.

He smiled as he recalled how … pleasant? … wonderful? … good—he'd decided that was the right word—it had been. It had been *good* working the project with her. It had taken three months, and they'd completed it a month prior. It had turned out so much better than he'd anticipated. He hadn't expected to like it. What would there be to like? It was Marla's kitchen, a place filled with utilitarian equipment for meal preparation and dealing with the associated mess. That's how he'd looked at it.

The only thing he hated more than shopping was selecting the endless design features for a project like kitchen remodeling. Marla agonized endlessly over each miniscule detail.

At the start of the process, while she considered every conceivable kind of window to place in the fifteen-by-thirteen-foot extension, which would add room for a round table to seat eight, he read a book on his iPhone. Before they set off to select material for countertops, he downloaded a new book.

At the factory, they'd had to put on hard hats to enter the warehouse, where aisles and aisles of four-by-eight-foot slabs of granite, marble, and synthetic imitations of the two stood on end in display stalls. They'd only moved three stalls away from the doorway when Marla had stopped and ran her hand over a granite sample.

"This one's a possibility."

The salesperson, Donna, was tall, blond, and comely. The hem of her dress stopped two inches above her knees, and a tiny hard hat sat atop her beauty shop do. She made a note on her clipboard.

Willie glanced at the mottled pattern of dark and light brown dots and thought, *Whatever.*

"Our present kitchen," Marla told Donna, "is black and white. Modern. Cold. I want our new kitchen to feel warm."

They walked the length of the warehouse and were halfway back to the starting point when Donna stopped them. "How about this one?"

Willie looked up from the iBook he'd been reading as he trailed the shoppers. Donna's slab had one corner filled with the same mottled pattern Marla liked at the start, but the rest was medium dark brown with fine striation lines running the length of the piece.

Whoa!

A vision of how to employ those slabs formed.

"Can I borrow your clipboard?" he asked.

Donna handed it over, and he flipped to the second page of the yellow legal-size pad. He sketched a layout of the counters in Marla's kitchen.

"See," Willie said. "We lay the panels such that this mottled portion of three slabs meets here, above the dishwasher. And the rest of the countertops are all the line effect. I think if the whole countertop were done with the mottled pattern, a person's eyes would say, 'This is kind of nice.' But, if we use this one"—Willie rapped his knuckle on the striations—"the lines will draw the eye around the kitchen. Kind of like encouraging the eyeballs to take in the whole room at once. See what I'm saying?"

He handed the clipboard to Donna. She glanced from sketch to sample slab, back and forth a couple of times. She frowned. "I have to tell you that it'll take an extra slab to do what you've drawn. But if that's what you want, no problem."

"I don't think so," Marla said. "If we work this like a sewing pattern with a bolt of cloth ..."

He'd surprised her—in a pleasant way for once. No question. The way she stopped talking, looked at him, put her hands on her hips, smiled, and shook her head.

Willie stayed in front of *his* slab of granite and read as Donna and Marla meandered through the rest of the warehouse. When they finished, they returned to Willie. Marla flashed such a stirring smile at him, he shifted his weight from one foot to the other and crossed his hands in front of his crotch.

Donna smirked and rolled her eyes.

Willie blushed.

The next day, the two went to the contractor's offices to pick out wood for the kitchen cabinets.

"Oak," Marla said.

"You want the result to be warm," Willie said. "Look at these oak samples. They're not cold, but they are loud and kind of shout at you, 'I am Oak,' in a manly baritone. How about this cherrywood? See. It's softer. Feminine. It speaks in the alto range. See the red tones? Warm. Warm and nice. These hard, dark grains in the oak diminish the warm effect."

Marla was clearly more astonished and clearly more pleased with him than she'd been the day before. And last night. But Willie kept his thoughts pure. He didn't want to be embarrassed in front of the sales*man* as he had been the day before by the sales*woman*.

Willie found himself participating willingly in selecting the rest of the features of not *her* kitchen, as he'd originally considered it, but *their* kitchen. It was a small project, compared to what he'd managed before. And the way the contractor organized it, they only had one major decision to make a day. No pressure at all.

And he'd enjoyed—no, way more than enjoyed—working with Marla.

Collaborating on the remodeling project had turned out to be just as he'd imagined marriage to Marla would be all those years ago, when he'd fallen in love with her.

After their second date, he'd personalized the biblical phrasing—he, Willie, would leave his father and mother, and he would cling to Marla, and the two would become one flesh, one mind, one heart, one soul. He didn't tell her of the depth of his feelings for her for months. He didn't want to frighten her off. But when the senior class rings arrived, he gave his to her.

"I want to go steady with you. I hope it leads to us becoming engaged and to us being married."

When it did, life with Marla turned out to be just as he'd imagined. Wondrous. One flesh, one soul. It ran that way all through the honeymoon.

Then the US Navy had demanded attention because of the exorbitant salary it paid Willie. After thirty-four years and retirement with an admiral's star, he'd landed a management position in the aerospace industry. There, he'd displayed a talent for digging troubled divisions out of a hole.

In April, he'd retired from a Seattle-based job as a vice president with blood pressure and pulse rate a tweak short of hypertension. Mandatory retirement at age sixty-five had saved his life, Willie was convinced.

While he was in Seattle, Marla had stayed in Missouri. Her mother was in a home there. After five damned years living apart and working twenty damned hours a day on the damned program, he figured it would be great to be married again.

And it had been great for most of April. They'd made love like newlyweds for a week and like they were comfortable being married to each other after that. She surprised him. She seemed to be interested in intimacy.

April had been a fine month. He'd exercised, eaten more of the right things, and drank less of the wrong ones. They'd walked together and talked.

During the second week in May, he'd begun taking his last cup of morning coffee to the patio in back. Their house sat on a hill overlooking the Mississippi and Missouri Rivers floodplain. Across the low land, bluffs rose dark on the Illinois side of the Father of Waters between the confluences of the Illinois and Missouri Rivers. The bluffs stood perhaps five or six crow-flight miles away, but it looked to Willie like they were much farther away. The notion that he could see a long way across land where people were busy doing things that he no longer had to work himself near to death over sat comfortably on the mornings with the heady aroma of his Italian roast coffee rising on tendrils of steam from his mug. The view, the coffee, the solitary contemplation of the complementary pair puddled mellow in his head.

May came. It brought anticipated flowers and her commitments, unanticipated. He should have anticipated them. The Christmas letter, which he wrote each year after considerable flogging, had a paragraph about them. He wrote about her work at the parish grade school; her sewing club; and the four charities she gave time, sewing projects, and donations to. Perhaps if he hadn't been coerced into writing the Christmas letter and her activities, he would have remembered them. But, too, if it hadn't been for the coercion, the letter would not have been written. So he'd wound up being surprised by how much she was gone.

He should have paid attention, should have been aware of the time required for her activities, should have realized she too had a job, jobs. He sighed. *Mea culpa, mea maxima culpa.*

He spent his time on things he'd had no time for before. *New York Times* crosswords, done with an ink pen, and sudoku filled his mornings and afternoons with a self-indulgent, decadent sense of arrival at a place he'd been striving to get to all his life. She, however, viewed his wallowing in leisure activities through a full workday as hedonism, communism, or some other -ism that undercut everything she worked so hard to accomplish with her awake hours. She hadn't been crazy about his "games" back in May. But she loathed them by June.

June was also the month she'd told him she wanted to build a new house.

"What's wrong with this one?"

"Everything!"

He'd had a bellyful of major projects at his last job and hated the notion of diving into a new one. Picking out all the crap that goes into a build-a-house-from-scratch project appealed less than a tooth extraction without Novocain. Extracting what she really wanted was pulling hen's teeth, but he finally got it. What she really wanted was an eating area off the kitchen large enough for a round table with seating for eight.

"Well, all right then," he'd gushed. "We'll add on."

She'd acquiesced, but he sensed it would have been better if he could have orchestrated it so it had been her idea and a lot better if he hadn't enthused over killing her original project.

Still, once they'd gotten into the project, it had turned out to be one of those rare precious times that a man recollected memories of at unexpected moments—moments when it dawned on him that he'd been blessed gloriously in his life on earth. That day he'd fallen in love with Marla. When she'd agreed to go steady with him. Their wedding day ... and night. The births of their three children. That special week they'd shared in Hong Kong when he'd been the commanding officer of an aircraft carrier on a port visit there. The month after he'd retired from the Seattle job. The kitchen remodeling project.

As they'd worked the project, it had become *their* kitchen. He smiled recalling how great it had felt to partner with his wife on the design. They'd worked together as if they really were one flesh, one mind, one artistic soul creating a kitchen masterpiece.

But then, the project was completed, and it was as if he were a positron and she an electron and the nuclear force holding them together in an atom had suddenly vanished. The remodeling project had been holding them together.

Did that mean nothing else bound them to each other?

That morning, before she walked in, he'd been thinking about their collaborative effort and marveling over what they'd created together—their kitchen. And it was warm and delicious thinking. He hadn't been thinking about how quickly arguments escalated to anger recently.

Only warm and delicious thoughts had filled his head. Then Marla had walked into *her* kitchen, and it had all gone to hell.

He pushed off from the counter, walked around the round table—with seating for six without the leaf—and stared out the window at gray. Low-lying, light gray fog covered the floodplain. The air was gray with haze and mist, but he could still see to the Mississippi, where thick, darker gray clouds had formed above the river and obscured the bluffs. Up was blue. Horizontal was gray.

Gray.

Depressing. Still, things had calmed down enough so he could think a little.

He always stood while he ate breakfast, or "scarfed it," she said, shaking her head. For years, he'd gobbled breakfast and hopped to it—to avoid, "Burnin' daylight, Pilgrims," as the Duke would say.

Besides having done breakfast that way for years, decades, actually, there was another reason to scarf and get out of there. The kitchen might be their kitchen when Marla wasn't in it. But when she was there, that kitchen was hers. When she was there, he could not stand anywhere without being in her way. If he moved, he moved to the spot she intended going to next. It was the same as shouting, "Get the hell out of my kitchen!"

The first time he'd realized she guarded her territory like an alpha female wolf was eleven, no, twelve years prior. He'd retired from the US Navy and was looking for a job—carefully and deliberately. They'd gone for a late-morning walk and were both fixing lunch for themselves in the small kitchen of their rental house. They'd kept bumping into each other, which he found pleasant. She, however, had done the arms akimbo thing, which in effect said, "Listen here, Buster," though she really said, "I married you for better or for worse, but not for lunch."

It had rocked him back for a moment. Then he knew where that had come from. It did not sound like Marla at all. It sounded like Irma. It sounded exactly like Irma.

Marla regarded Irma as her best friend. The two women wrote to each other once a week, and Irma phoned periodically. Beginning with her second marriage, she didn't worry about the cost of long-distance minutes.

"Irma!" He'd snarled and thrown his half-made sandwich in the trash, gone upstairs, cranked up his job search, and lined up an interview with McDonnell Douglas in St. Louis the following week.

Irma!

The root of his troubles. That soulless gold digger. After twelve years of marriage, her first husband, Gene, had died of lung cancer. A year later, she'd married Arnold. Two years after that, she'd divorced him and gotten a big house and a new Lexus out of the deal. Three years after that, she'd married Ben. That one had lasted five years, at which point she'd unburdened Ben from carrying so much wealth around all by himself.

Irma. Marla always listened to her.

The sun, weakened by haze and wisps of fog, finally managed to burn away enough of the gray obscurant so he could see the top of the Illinois bluffs. Thick fog rising off the river still obscured most of the cliffs. He returned to the coffeepot and topped off. It would be nice to watch the rest of the steadfast, geologic feature emerge from the fog. He'd come to think of the bluffs as his own personal, local Gibraltar.

All very interesting history, but it doesn't get to the cause of the blowup this morning.

As he put the coffeepot back on the heated base, the doorbell ding-donged.

Had Marla ordered something from Amazon? Generally, she needed his help on the computer to complete a purchase.

Yeah, he thought, *so I wind up using my credit card instead of hers.*

He took his mug with him. It wasn't FedEx he saw through the glassed front door. It was Irma.

He wouldn't see her for weeks at a time. When he did, she always amazed him. Her straight, fire-engine hair was cut just below her ears. A thirty-five-year-old would kill to have Irma's face and lithe body. And her pantsuit conveyed, "This is casual wear, but it cost ten thousand dollars."

He unlocked and opened the door and stared at her. She glared back at him. Suddenly, she grabbed the mug from his hand, sloshed coffee on his shoes and entryway tile, and threw the mug into the front yard. Then she stepped inside and grabbed his arm

135

and pulled him toward the bathroom between the two upstairs bedrooms.

"What the hell are you doing?"

Irma didn't let up on his arm. In the bathroom, she flicked on the light and positioned him in front of the mirror.

"Look at yourself," she ordered.

He did. Then he frowned at the hard face glowering back at him.

No mystery about where the face had come from. He'd cultivated it, had practiced it in the mirror when he shaved so he could wear it to work every morning.

Almost four years ago now, his project team had won a major Defense Department contract after two years of intense competition. Then they'd had to deliver on the promises they'd made. Staffing had ramped from twenty-five core personnel on the capture team to two thousand in six months. Those first management team meetings had been total chaos. Ideas had been winged all over the page. And as soon as a decision was taken, somebody would point out why it couldn't work.

One day, one of the guys had posted a large sign on the conference room wall. "Nobody is as Dumb as All of Us," the sign had proclaimed.

That had been a wake-up call for Willie. He hadn't known how to move such a program into execution. His team had experience with previous projects. They had to propose ideas, options, and ways to move forward effectively, efficiently, and economically. And fast. Then, out of the options, the team had to pick the best one to execute. But they were all over the page.

The next morning, with vestiges of shaving cream still on his face, he had addressed his visage. "We need to impose order. We need to have a process." He'd glared at his image. "We need to be a hard-ass."

For a moment, the plural and singular incompatibility in the last statement had given him pause.

The lips on the face in the mirror had pressed together into a thin, short, straight line. The eyes had burned blue and hard and cold, like looking into a crack in a glacier. "We are a hard-ass," he'd said to the mirror. Looking back at Willie was indeed a hard-ass.

He'd looked away, letting his face relax. Then he'd reassembled the look and checked the result.

Sheesh.

What a joke. While watching his image, he'd remanufactured the look he wanted. He'd paid attention to how it felt to hold that pose. Then he'd turned away, relaxed his face, reposed, and rechecked. After the seventh iteration, he had two in a row that satisfied him.

He'd exulted, "By George! He's got it!" Which immediately worried him.

He'd looked away, did his drill again, and checked again. Looking back was the hard-ass. And Willie controlled him.

Later, he'd walked into the usual morning meeting cacophony of voices. He hadn't taken his seat, as he usually did, but had remained standing behind his chair. After a moment, one of the women seated opposite Willie had noticed his angry glower and pointed it out to her neighbor. The neighbor had nudged his neighbor, and silence had grown from a local puddle and rolled around the table in both directions, like sports fans doing "the wave" at an arena.

The silence had achieved completeness and filled the room. Willie let it ferment. Fidgeting started and the leader of the production team dropped a pen on the table. Willie swung rattlesnake eyes on him and froze the production guy's limbs as a real snake would have frozen a mouse dinner. The manager's Adam's apple bobbed up and then down again.

"These morning meetings are nothing but a Mongolian goat

rope," Willie growled. "My fault entirely. Through yesterday, it was my fault we weren't getting anywhere. We need to change some things. This is what we are going to do. The morning meeting will start at six instead of seven—starting tomorrow. We will have an afternoon meeting at five. That starts today."

Willie expected someone to voice an objection and hoped it would be the production manager. Production was a long ways into the future. He could afford to fire the man and get a replacement. Willie hungered for any meager excuse to fire someone. Apparently, his team had good survival instincts.

They watched as Willie walked to the bulletin board, pulled down "Nobody is as Dumb as All of Us," and tacked up, "Nobody is as Smart as All of Us."

"None of us," he said, "can do his or her job alone. If engineering runs into trouble, it is not just engineering's problem but certainly production's and everyone else's on the management team's as well."

Willie walked back and sat.

"We need each other. I need you. I am nothing without you. But, make no mistake. I am not your friend."

And he swept his practiced look around the table. Willie knew even the ones seated next to him got the full message. Even if they couldn't see Willie's face directly, they could see the effects of what the ones' across the table saw. The looks on their faces eloquently conveyed the message.

"We need ideas. We will listen to ideas for thirty minutes in the morning meeting. Then we will discuss which ideas to put into our plans. After fifteen minutes of that, we will make decisions. Then we will go to work. In the afternoon, we will review the decisions we made in the morning and decide if we need to adjust."

He locked his reptile eyes on each person around the table for a moment.

Then he said, "We need ideas. We are going around the table. I want to hear your ideas. If you don't have ideas about how to organize this project, then you don't belong in this meeting." He swiveled his hard eyes to the woman across from him. "Isabel, start. Ideas. What do you have?"

Two and a half months later, the government program management team had conducted a progress review. Every program-health parameter they'd measured had been green.

"See?" Irma asked, jerking him out of four years ago and plopping him in the present.

The most chagrined-looking hard-ass he'd ever seen looked at Willie from the mirror.

"Men can be such boobs," Irma said.

Willie glanced at the reflection of hers.

Irma rolled her eyes and sidled behind him. "What she sees in you …" she mumbled. A moment later, the front door slammed behind her.

Willie remembered it then. He'd been leaning on the counter admiring *their* kitchen. Marla had opened the door, surprising him. She'd irritated him by opening the door and claiming full possession, total ownership of *her* kitchen. And he saw the look she had seen on his face.

That face could sit on the face of a man who'd hit a woman.

Willie remembered his Oak Ridge Boys CD, *The Definitive Collection*. There was song on there about smiling. There it was. Track 19. "Everyday."

Willie brought his portable player to the bathroom and cranked up the Boys; then he and the mirror went to work on a new face.

Newbie

FNG.

After eleven years in the United States Navy, that's what I was, still, again—a fairly new guy. Of course, the other guys had another word for the F. Anyway, I was getting kinda close to really sorta peeved about still being an FNG.

On the other hand, if I forced myself to look at my situation, I could get kinda close to really sort of admitting I was still an FNG through my own darned fault.

I'd enlisted right after high school. The navy had sent me to Electronics Technician School following boot camp. My plan had been to serve my four-year obligation, get out of the service, land a good job, find a five-foot—so I wouldn't have to look up to her—Marilyn Monroe to marry, have a son and a daughter, and live happily ever after. It was a great plan—until I signed up for a navy college program, with an additional obligation, of course. I graduated and received an officer's commission, and then, when I was down to two years of owed service, I decided I wanted to fly navy jets.

Sometimes it's hard to listen to people, even when they're right, even if it's yourself trying to talk sense into you.

What mattered though, Everett Novak was tired of being an

FNG and tired of being considered such by guys with less than half his time in the navy.

In the Warhorses squadron, the FNG carried Newbie as his call sign. The only way to get rid of it was to hand it over to the next FNG to check aboard. I'd carried the bloody moniker since August. And it wasn't just a name. It was a way of being treated. In the Warhorses, an FNG ain't squat.

I thought about baptism day.

In the Warhorses squadron, JOPA (Junior Officer Protective Association) automatically awarded membership to lieutenants and below. The enrollment included twelve names, besides mine, Newbie. Specifically and especially excluded were the CO and XO, three lieutenant commander department heads, and three ground pounders. The pounders were junior officers. But because they were earthbound mortals, not pilots, they did not qualify for membership.

The High Hooba-Jooba Senior Junior Bubba was Dose. Dose had black hair except for the circle of white above his left ear, which supposedly could be caused by a dose of VD. He wore his name as proudly as he would have worn a Distinguished Flying Cross. He had completed two deployments to Nam, and ordinarily, he would have transferred to a shore duty job after the second, but he'd extended for a third combat tour.

His first stint to Nam had come in 1968. The carrier had just arrived in the Tonkin Gulf when LBJ had announced the bombing halt over North Vietnam. Dose was crushed. He had wanted to bomb the North as much as he'd wanted his name, Newbie, to go away. But the Newbie name would not, could not go away from him by wishing it away.

Dose (but Newbie then) even had an idea for something more respectable—Hoser, as in hosing the flying enemies of the United States from the sky with streams of machine-gun bullets. But among the things he learned that first cruise was that the call sign you wound up with, the nickname that would stick to you like a booger on your finger, came from JOPA. Dose endured the first cruise dropping bombs on trees, bombing craters into dirt roads that a gomer could fill in two minutes with the shovel from a kid's toy to take to the beach, and he'd slogged through a second tour of more of the same stupid missions.

Dose became the head of JOPA at the beginning of his second cruise. He was more than comfortable with the roll by the time I checked aboard.

The USS *Marianas* was off the coast of Southern California, beginning the last phase of training prior to deploying. After flight ops secured at midnight, Dose called a JOPA meeting to order and promptly assigned me my call sign.

"Newbie!"

I glared at Dose with my evil eye, which is the right one. "I've been in the Nav for eleven years, I'm senior to you, and I had a tour to Nam—"

I cut off verbalizing the thought trail I was following: I'd been to Nam before, and I'd gotten a Bronze Star and a Commendation Medal for combat actions. Tooting your own horn slathered you with communal disdain. Nobody told me that, but I could feel it happen as my mouth motored away. My biggest sin was confessing that I had served in the surface navy. Surface navy guys were floating, earthbound mortals. My face felt hot, and I started sweating as I slammed my mouth shut.

It was quiet inside the junior officer bunkroom. Noise from the ventilation blowers outside the room seemed to create walls every bit as solid as the sheets of aluminum bounding the space. Twelve sets of eyes had me nailed. I tried to swallow but was out of spit. Dose smiled and held up an index finger.

"One Stupid Dollar for arguing about your name." He held up a second finger and then flicked up a third.

"Three dollars! What for?"

Dose reignited his smile and held up four fingers.

Red was the treasurer. He got up from the bunk he was sitting on and held his hand out to me.

"I presume you're done committing fineable stupidities," Red said pleasantly.

"Welcome aboard, (insert obscene name here)," the twelve bellowed. Apparently, an obscenity is a JOPA-approved variation to Newbie.

At subsequent JOPA assemblies, I learned a few things about flying in combat from Dose. AAA—anti-aircraft artillery or flak—for instance. He described a clip of tracer .37 mm as a string of five red tennis balls rising up to float past your airplane. A quad barrel .23 mm looked like a bucket of sparks hurled up from the ground. According to Dose, gomer flak wasn't really an attempt to blow a plane out of the sky. Those tracer rounds were communicating with us, telling us, "After your tons and tons of bombs, we are still down here. We will still be here when you are gone, and there's not one bloody thing you can do about it."

Most of the time, I didn't much care for Dose—too much I'm-head-of-JOPA attitude for my taste. I did appreciate the combat lessons he passed on, even if he did it because he liked to hear himself speak more than he cared about protecting the newbie. And at times I admired his wit—like when he paraphrased the secretary of defense's majorly stupid comment from the early days of the war. "We're not bombing North Vietnam; we're communicating with them." And, too, Dose'd signed up for a third tour because he was still anxious to drop five-hundred-pound communication devices on North Vietnam, and he was hopeful that Nixon might still inject common sense into the dicked-up war. In that way, we were alike. If there was a war going on, we both felt compelled to be a part of it.

I couldn't say what underlay Dose's motivation. Mine derived from the antiwar protestors. In my mind, they were anti-America more than antiwar. They were the reason I put in for flight training. They made Dose and me blood brothers.

All that being said, being Newbie still sucked.

My welcome-aboard JOPA meeting had occurred near the end of August off the coast of California. I had just joined the squadron. September was spent completing preparations for a seven-month deployment to the Tonkin Gulf. Crossing the Pacific consumed October. November and early December had been spent on Yankee Station turning South Vietnamese and Laotian trees into toothpicks with five-hundred-pounders. But I had thirty-five combat missions in my logbook by the time we left the Tonkin Gulf to spend the holidays in Yokosuka, Japan.

Christmas Eve in Japan. Christmas sucked. Nothing on God's earth is more depressing than Christmas on a military base. At least, that's how I saw it. It was worse than being Newbie.

The thing is, I'd actually married someone better than any Marilyn—five-foot-two Katy. She was a wholesome, attractive brunette. And miracle of miracles, she was almost as fond of me as I was of her. Together, we'd made a girl baby and a boy. But they were in San Diego. I was in a junior officer bunkroom in the USS *Marianas*, which was tied to a pier in Yokosuka, Japan.

Christmas probably doesn't suck this bad in godless, communist North Vietnam.

American POWs in Hanoi snowplowed into my mind. Guilt, major Catholic-nuns-for-grade-and-high school teachers-inspired guilt cut through my complaints. I was whining over my plight. Some of those guys had been there a long time. Alvarez. He was on his seventh Christmas Eve in a Hanoi prison.

Apologizing to the POWs, I got out my letter-writing kit. The top of my box held eight-by-ten photos—Katy in one, four-year-old Jessica with her hand on the shoulder of younger brother, Jeffrey, in the other. I propped my family on the desk. It was more than pictures of them. I remembered an old cowboy movie. An Indian chief did not want his picture taken. He was afraid the camera box would capture his soul. The chief might have been right. The one of Katy belied the notion that beauty is only skin-deep. The essence of her personhood looked back at me from the photo. Sure as shooting, Katy was a fine, fine person—of the female persuasion—packaged in a luscious, smooth, soft—

The door to the JOB ripped open. Tiny barged in.

"Newbie," Tiny bellowed, "JOPA mandatory meeting at the O Club. Climb into some civvies. Let's go."

Tiny was the biggest guy in the squadron and the only one who didn't rag on me for being short. I liked him. Not then, though.

"No thanks. I am not in an O Club frame of mind."

"Newbie, listen. You contributed a lot of Stupid Bucks to the party fund. Get some of it back. And this isn't a matter for debate." He held up a fist and pulled up the little finger. "JOPA mandatory." He pulled up other fingers as he ticked off reasons for me to go to the club. "Two, Christmas Eve. Three, sitting here alone feeling sorry for yourself. Four, you're Newbie, and it's JOPA mandatory."

"You said the last one already."

"Either you put your civvies on, or I'll put them on you."

A deeper, darker mood than the one I'd just clawed out of gripped my ankles and pulled me back into the pit of despair.

Tiny grasped my left biceps and jerked me up.

"All right. All right," I said.

I touched Katy, sighed, put her and the kids away, stood up, yanked off my uniform *trou,* jammed legs into pants, and bitch grumbled.

Tiny sniggered.

"Newbies need an organization to protect them from JOPA."

Tiny laughed his ass off.

When we got to the club, we found JOPA seated at a round table, large enough to accommodate twelve. Dog Lips had the duty. He had the duty every day of the in-port period. Dog Lips. His call sign could have been the Joker. He was always pulling something. The last night on the line, he targeted the CO. Most of the guys would have been bummed to be restricted to the ship the whole time in port, especially when you appreciated the arithmetic. It had been fifty-two days since the *Marianas* had been in port when it tied up in Yokosuka. It would be fifty days until the next port when we left for another stint with the Tonkin Gulf Yacht Club. To Dog Lips, however, no price was too much to pay for pulling off a really good prank.

The CO flew a bombing hop over Laos the last night on the line. He didn't wear glasses except for night landings on the carrier. The CO's night flight routine was to check his flight and survival gear, clean his glasses and stuff them in a pocket on his torso harness, and leave the equipment on his ready-room chair while he visited the head. Dog Lips waited until the CO left. He took the glasses and drew a grease-pencil profile shot of a busty female on each lens with the boobs pointing at each other. Then he replaced the glasses.

After the bombing mission, the CO, as was his habit, put his glasses on as he began his descent from holding behind the ship. He claimed those damned boobs almost locked his eyes into a cross-eyed state. As he descended, he frantically tried to clean the glasses but only smeared them. So he shot his landing without them and got a poor landing grade. He had held the highest average landing grade of all the air wing pilots for the line period. That night's grade bumped him down to number three.

JOPA, with the exception of myself, a no-account newbie, was amused. Everyone else in the squadron, the heavies, and the enlisted sailors, hated to see the CO PO'ed. JOPA, however, was amused. Dog Lips had borne his punishment with irrepressible good spirits. I bore mine with an undisguised prickly demeanor as we took the last two empty chairs at the table.

Dose looked at me for a moment. I glared back at him.

"Well," Dose said. "JOPA all present or accounted for. First order of business, a toast to Dog Lips. Tiny, Newbie, pour yourselves a beer."

There were two pitchers in the middle of the table. Tiny poured for me and then himself. Dose lifted his glass.

"To Dog Lips."

Everyone lifted his glass. Not me.

"What the hell, Newbie?" Dose asked. "Drink or pay a Stupid Buck."

"What Dog Lips did, it was dangerous and stupid," I said.

I pulled out my wallet, threw a twenty on the table. "Let me know when that runs out," I said.

Dose looked down at the bill and then up and into my eyes.

"Newbie, Dog Lips pulled the joke on the one guy in the squadron who could handle it. That's what made it so funny."

"It was dangerous and stupid," I said.

"War is dangerous. This one is stupid, the way it's being run. Dog Lips's prank contributed to the esprit of JOPA."

"The world according to Dose. What it did was drive the gap between JOPA and the rest of the squadron wider. Hell yes, war is dangerous. Most wars have stupid times, this one more than most, maybe. If those things are true, the squadron ought to pull together, not just the JOPA part of it."

I threw another twenty onto the table, and I left.

"Newbie, get your ass back here."

I smiled as I walked away from Dose and his adulators.

The spring-loaded door closed behind me. Then it opened again.

"Goddamn it, Newbie."

It was Dose. I kept walking.

He grabbed my left biceps and stopped me. I pivoted and drove my right fist onto his breastbone. It would hurt, but it wouldn't *hurt* him—at least that's the way I figured it. He sat on his butt on the sidewalk rubbing his chest and mumbling with frequently distinguishable *f* words.

"You'd be well advised to not get back up just yet," I said.

He shut up and rubbed some more. I turned, and my righteous indignation propelled me back toward the ship.

I took deep breaths, held them, and let them out. Adrenalin didn't turn itself off like a faucet. It coasted down.

Overcast above. Ahead, a streetlight melted a fuzzy hole in the dark and illuminated a circle of sidewalk and blacktop and a vertical arch on a metal-sided shed. Feeling came back. Hands sticking out of the sleeves of an inadequate jacket didn't feel the chill as much as the skin under my clothes felt it. My heels hit the pavement without making a sound. It seemed to be too cold for sound or smell. I *handkerchiefed* a drip off the end of my nose.

No taste of beer on my tongue. I knew how it would have gone if I'd started drinking. I had let it happen to me twice before. Anguish obliterates restraint. Booze becomes water. Oblivion would come first, followed by puking, followed by a just-let-me-die-God hangover. But He doesn't. And then there's guilt, which doesn't feel all that different from the anguish, which started the cycle to begin with.

See, Newbie, even the clouds of a Japanese overcast on Christmas Eve have a silver lining.

As I climbed the ladder to board the carrier, my stomach grumbled. I hadn't felt like eating. There was an around-the-clock burger grill open on the third deck when we were at sea. It would be a Christmas miracle if it were open in port.

But it was. A third of the crew was aboard for duty. On deployment, carriers had to be prepared for an emergency call to get underway and steam to some new or old trouble spot needing the application of five-hundred-pound communication devices, otherwise known as Mark 82 bombs.

A double cheeseburger. I took a bite.

Happy birthday, Baby Jesus.

Swallow and bite.

Merry Christmas, Katy …

The lump in my throat hurt, and there I was with a cheek-bulging mouthful.

"Everett."

The CO was standing next to my table.

"May I?"

He pointed at the seat next to me.

"Oh, *yeshir.*"

I looked to see if I had spit food on the table. Didn't see anything. I gulped it down.

"Seems like a long time since anyone called me by my name, Skipper."

The CO leaned on his elbows and clasped his hands together on the tabletop.

"You and Dose had a falling out."

"How did you—"

"I was there with the XO, department heads, and the ground officers. We were having dinner in a back room at the club."

"I hit him."

"Did you intend to punch him in the chest?"

"If I'd hit him on the jaw, I could have really hurt him."

"You didn't want to do that?"

I shook my head.

The CO got up from beside me and walked around the four-place table and sat across from me.

"Everett, a lot of people think this is a dicked-up war. Fact is, all war is dirty, messy, dicked-up business. Not many of us can find a best way to handle it. The way I see it, this country was born out of war and has been in big and little ones almost continuously since then. In all our history, we've only had three presidents I consider to be worth a damn at running a war—Truman, FDR, and Abe. So dicked-up-ed-ness is the norm."

He stopped talking and held my eyes. I looked away. I couldn't think looking into his blue eyes. What he said about war. I nodded. The presidents. I thought about all the other ones, the ones he didn't mention. I nodded again. I looked back up into the skipper's eyes. He was waiting for me to get it; that's what I thought.

When I looked at him, I always thought, *outside linebacker.* He had close-cropped, black hair; a swarthy complexion; and a normal sort of nose. I pictured Dog Lips's glasses sitting on his honker. I felt my face smile.

He smiled. For an instant.

"Now listen up, Everett. The Warhorses is a combat unit—a unit, not a bunch of loosely packaged Lone Rangers. Here's what's going to happen. Tomorrow morning, Dog Lips will move out of the room he shares with Dose. He will move into the junior officer bunkroom. You will move in with Dose."

I sat back.

"Your mouth's hanging open."

I closed it.

"Dose is the top dog among junior officers, and someone has to be on the bottom. You don't seem to want your assigned role. I do not care if you and Dose work it out. I do not care if you kill each other. I do not care if one of you kills the other. What I do care about is that, by the time the *Marianas* launches its first combat sorties in January, my squadron is a unified war-fighting organization."

He stood and I started to. He reached across the table, put a paw on my shoulder, and I sat.

"Merry Christmas, Everett."

"Um, you too, Skipper."

The burger was cold. It didn't matter. When I finished eating, I thanked the cook, Seaman Sanchez, "For the finest Christmas Eve dinner I've had all year."

He laughed as if humor was hard to come by.

Back in the bunkroom, I opened the fold-down desk lid. The halves of two torn-in-half twenties lay there. Whatever it meant, it didn't matter. It was 2300. I still had an hour of Christmas Eve to spend with my family.

Darling, Daddy, Dead Vietcong Maker*

Stretch hesitated by his commanding officer's door. He raised his hand to knock. *Wham!* Pause. Then he felt the jolt. It took a second for the catapult shock to transmit through the tons of aircraft-carrier steel. *Wham.* The ship had just shot the first two planes of the next launch from the bow catapult.

Before, when he'd heard and felt a cat shot, he'd wanted to be the lucky bastard who got to fly. Even on a black-assed night in crappy weather when no sane man volunteered and everyone stayed clear of the ready room because the schedule officer might need a pilot for a pop-up flight, he'd had the Pavlovian reaction.

That was before. He'd tried to prevent it, but he'd become like the rest of them. The other junior pilots had two moralities. At work they swore, belched, farted, and turned enemies into *crispy critters*. On deployment, they avoided saloons with spittoons as being overly civilized. Before going home, they unzipped their work morality like a flight suit and hung it on a hook in a locker.

At home, his squadron mates became, "Darling, take the garbage out, please." "Daddy, Daddy, look at my drawing." "Son, my Rotary is looking for a speaker."

It won't happen to me. That's what he thought. Navy

fighter-bomber pilot Stretch and Stretch the husband of Teresa and father of four-year old Jennifer and two-year old Edgar Jon were the same person. He needed one morality to guide the two aspects of his life. Now he wished he had two moralities, because his morality had become a heartless, reptilian, soulless, son-of-a-bitch one.

The cats continued to fire, and LBJ popped into his mind. He'd been in flight training four years ago. On the ten o'clock news, the pres had announced he would not seek reelection. He would end the nation's war in Vietnam. Stretch had prayed, *Please, God, don't let the war end before I get there.*

Stretch took a breath and knocked.

"Minute," the CO hollered.

The door jerked open. A smile bloomed. "Str— What's the matter?"

A lump of emotion as big and hard as a baseball stuck in Stretch's throat. He clamped his teeth on sissy noise, thrust out his left hand, and opened his fist.

The CO looked down at the wings on Stretch's palm.

"What happened?"

He cleared his throat. "Just take it, sir, please."

The CO's call sign was Bear. He was six two and thick across the chest and shoulders and had black, bushy eyebrows and a low forehead. He looked like a bear. Stretch, on the other hand, was given a *tall* nickname because he was short.

Bear reached out a paw, grabbed the front of Stretch's flight suit, hauled him into the room, and slammed the door so hard it felt like another cat shot. He leaned down, inches from Stretch's face.

"I do not have the patience for one of these goddamn junior officer conversations, where extracting information is like pulling molars with goddamn eyebrow-plucking tweezers.

"Talk!"

Stretch tried to step back. He was against the door. "I was leading a four-plane."

"See, mouth works fine." The CO backed off, nodded. "Continue."

"We dumped our bombs in Laos. Uprooted trees. Made toothpicks. Halfway back across Nam, a forward air controller called. He had enemy troops in the open. We had our twenty-millimeter machine gun bullets left. 'Hustle,' the FAC said.

"We zorched low. I saw them. Bunch of VC hauling ass across an open field. I rolled in. Squeezed the trigger. Guns didn't fire. Number Two rolled in. He got a couple. The Ops O was Three. He nailed a few more. Four's guns jammed. I told him to climb and hold."

The CO hissed. "Half the damn guns jammed. Typical. Then what?"

"I came around again. A half dozen bad guys left. I turned my gun switch off and back on again. I wanted to kill those bastards."

"Jesus," the CO said and flopped onto his desk chair.

It was a commandment: Never, never turn the gun switch off and back on again. The machine-gun loading mechanism *could* ram a live bullet into another live bullet and blow the nose off the airplane. If that happened, the plane would be lost; the pilot would be dead. They both weighed the confession.

"So," the CO said, "the warning in the flight manual says recycling the switch *could* cause an explosion. You figured a guy as lucky as you wouldn't have a problem."

That wasn't quite the way he'd looked at things, but Stretch nodded. It was close enough.

"That it?" the CO asked.

Stretch shook his head. "Two and the Ops O made a second run and killed all but one guy. I recycled that gun switch three,

155

maybe four times and rolled in again. I pulled the trigger kind of far out, so I'd have time to cycle it once more in the run. It wouldn't fire. I cycled it. It still wouldn't shoot."

Commandment two: Don't mess with switches in the middle of bombing or strafing runs. When diving at the earth at 450 knots, distractions are deadly.

"How close you come to flying into the ground?" the CO asked.

"Not very. I bottomed at 275 feet."

"Goddamn." The CO stood, rubbed his hand over his face, and sat back down. "Okay, here's what I want you—"

"No, sir. Just take them." He held out the wings, again.

"Listen to me—"

The little man dropped his wings on the corner of the big man's desk. "Sorry, CO." Stretch walked out.

The maintenance officer, Lieutenant Commander Hightower, had just returned to his room after a shower. The phone rang. It was the CO. Hightower listened; said, "Aye, Skipper"; hung up; and dressed. He found Stretch all the way aft in the hangar bay, port side, working a speed bag. Stretch was still in his flight suit, and sweat, tears, and snot ran down his face. He punched up at the bag furiously.

"Hey, Stretch," the MO shouted over the ever-present hangar bay cacophony of airplane repair noise—air-driven grinders, rivet guns, whistles from people moving planes. Next to the bag, a crew conducted a landing gear test. The hydraulic power unit whined, and landing gear went up, *clunk*, and down, *clunk*, and up, *clunk* …

Stretch kept punching. His lips parted like an alpha male wolf showing his teeth to a challenger. The MO grabbed his arm and pulled him away from the bag.

"Aw, man, look at your hands." The knuckles were bloody. "Stay," he said and walked over to the maintenance crew with the jacked airplane and got a handful of rags.

"Wipe your face." The MO handed him a rag.

The MO took Stretch by the arm and guided him to the balcony-like area just outboard of the speed bag. They sat on bitts, steel posts used to tie the carrier to a pier. "You're upset with yourself for being stupid, cycling the gun switch?"

The MO and the other heavies liked Stretch. Once, the CO had said, "Stretch listens. He doesn't understand what I want him to do flying wing—he asks questions until he gets it. Then he flies his position just like I told him to. Stretch is halfway close to a semisatisfactory junior officer."

"The real thing is," Stretch said, "I wanted to kill those VC so bad. Even if I was going to blow myself up, it didn't matter. Losing the navy's airplane, making Teresa a widow, never seeing my kids again—none of that mattered. I had to kill them." Stretch shook his head. "What the hell kind of person am I?"

They talked until the sun slipped down the cloudless, blue bowl of sky and the edge touched the surface of the South China Sea.

"Months and months of bombing trees, and is any of this doing any good?" the MO asked.

Stretch shook his head no, looked at his knuckles, and nodded yes.

The MO put his hand on Stretch's shoulder. "How about if we find the chaplain, ask him to hear your confession?" the MO asked.

"No!" Stretch shouted. He stood up, took a step forward, and put his hands on the waist-high lifelines.

The MO joined him. "Why not?"

"Because he'd *forgive* me."

The MO thought of My Lai, grimaced, and put his hand on Stretch's arm.

"Come on. Sit down."

"I quit."

The carrier started a turn to port. No need to look at his watch. The MO knew, five minutes until the next launch.

"I turned my wings in to the CO."

The MO reached into the breast pocket of his flight suit. "The CO said you dropped these by accident in his room."

The CO had actually said, "Take these to Stretch. Don't spend all night. If he won't pin 'em back on before next launch, throw 'em over the side." But Stretch didn't need to know that.

"Here's the deal," the MO said. "We're losing this war. After it's lost, our navy and nation will have to put things back together again."

"The navy'll be better off without a stupid, amoral asshole like me."

The MO slapped Stretch behind the head. "Your head won't let you commit mortal stupidities in an airplane ever again. I know it. You know it. What you did ripped a hunk of heart meat out of you. Your heart isn't going to let the beast from hell out of your belly ever again. You and I both know that too.

"The world keeps producing people you can't reason with, except with a five-hundred-pound bomb. When I'm back home, I want your head and your heart in control of the trigger finger and the thumb above the bomb pickle. That's what I want for my navy and for my country."

The MO held his hand out over the water and opened his fist.

"What's it going to be, Stretch? Take them back, or I drop them."

Stretch looked at his wings cupped in the MO's palm.

"Make up your mind. We missed dinner. I wanna get a burger."

Forwards

L ast week, I received an e-mail forward.

Actually, a goodly number of them hit my in-box, as happens most weeks.

Some people are annoyed by forwards, but they serve a number of purposes as far as I'm concerned. I keep track of a few buddies. *They're* getting old, and as long as their forwards come regularly, I know they are okay. Interesting snippets of little-known history come that way. Most days, political commentary shows up. The gist of these seems to be "We modern politicians pledge to make our sacred fortunes even bigger. Our sacred honor too will grow more glorious because we have power to define honor on Facebook and Twitter."

Forwarded obituaries, too, announced their arrival with a cheery "You have mail."

The obits concerned people I'd served with at some point in the military or worked with after I left the service. Many of them come months after the person's demise. These forwards began with an opening like "Holy crap! Just found out Skunk died last year." Both the forwarder and I had served with Skunk during Nam. Skunk had black hair and an apostrophe of white above his left ear. What else would anyone call him? And I'll admit—I'd read the forward about Skunk, and the others, and I'd say, "Darn.

Too bad." And I'd award Skunk a moment of silent sympathy. Then I'd get on with whatever I was doing.

The one I got last week from Combat Fats was different. I'd stayed in touch with Combat over the years. He'd joined our squadron flying missions over North Vietnam in 1972 as a fairly senior pilot. He'd been on the East Coast and had tried mightily to snag an assignment to a West Coast squadron, from where we deployed to the Tonkin Gulf, vice the Mediterranean, where the East Coast pukes went. He worried he wouldn't make it to the war before it ended. He was pudgy. What else were we going to call him? I always liked Fats—maybe because he'd prayed the same prayer I did. "Please, God, don't let the war end before I get there." I don't know when Combat had prayed his prayer, but I know when I prayed mine. It was the night LBJ announced he would not run for reelection. He would spend the rest of his time in office trying to get us out of Nam. At the time, I was in Meridian, Mississippi, just beginning two years of flight training. That night, watching the news, I'd prayed before I got up to turn off the TV.

While most of the rest of the world was praying for the war to end, Combat Fats and me had prayed for it to go on.

Combat and me had our prayer answered. During the North Vietnamese Easter Offensive in 1972, we flew our butts off, logging two or three combat missions a day. After the war, we both asked the same question: "If you have a prayer answered, shouldn't it feel like a blessing?"

We didn't have an answer, but we did mumble things at a glass of Jack Daniels like "The nation may have lost the war, but I sure as hell didn't lose my part." The other one of us would say, "Yeah. It was the pres and sec def lost it."

One subject we always migrated to in one of these sessions was the people we'd met and flown with. We'd extol their bravery and their pilot skills in both combat and bringing damaged planes back aboard the carrier at night and in crappy weather.

"Yeah. And did you ever notice what great women we married? So we weren't lucky in war, but were lucky in love," Combat had said once.

His wife had died a few years back, but he'd said stuff like that when she was alive too. Combat was one of the guys I tracked by forwards. They came, and it meant thumbs-up. Combat Fats was alive … and mostly well.

When that particular forward came from him, I didn't even look at the subject. I expected his thirty-five favorite puns; "a preacher, a plumber, and a pit bull walked into a bar" joke; or the like. I guess that's why the e-mail poleaxed me the way it did.

The original message was from Dog Lips.

Dog Lip's original read:

> None died last night. He and his wife Amanda Sue were entertaining. None'd been talking and laughing with a circle of guys, the way he did. Suddenly, he frowned, and then he collapsed to the floor. The way it went, aneurysm blew, man. Had to be.

None? *No way!* He wore the eternal young man's face. I had seen him two years ago, and if I'd had a Sherlock Holmes magnifying glass, I might've found a wrinkle. Combat Fat's forward pulled, not a memory, but at the patch of his soul that had *Velcroed* itself to mine the day I saw his face the first time.

May 27, 1972. Midday. Forty-five minutes before the carrier *Hancock* launched the second strike into North Vietnam that day. None was an FNG (fairly new guy) and a lieutenant (junior grade). He'd joined our squadron a few days before, but I was flying two and three hops a day and hadn't run into him. But I knew what name he got. Our CO liked to characterize junior officers by how many ass-kickings it took for a new guy to absorb a lesson. A one-ass-kick guy was exceptional. The CO said our newbie was a "no ass-kick junior officer." So he was called None.

That day, None was scheduled to make his first combat hop on that second go. I was an FOG (fairly old guy) and a lieutenant. I'd flown the first strike and was on the second too. After the brief, there was just time to scarf down some chow before man-up time on the flight deck. I ran to the pilots' dining room, grabbed a tray, hustled through the line, rushed to an empty spot at a table, plopped down, and shoveled food in with a fork in one hand and a spoon in the other. I was in a hurry.

My plane was spotted on cat one. They were going to shoot me first, so I was in a hurry. Or did I say that?

I might have made hog-snout-in-a-trough snuffling. I don't remember. I do remember feeling eyes on me. None sat across the table from me. His mouth hung open. My interpretation of the look his face wore: *Dear God in heaven, how long will it be before I act like that FOG?*

No time to ponder looks on newbie faces. I stood, smiled at None with the handle of the spoon sticking out of my mouth, and mumbled something. It might have been, "Good luck, Newbie. I hope you don't get your raggedy FNG ass shot full of holes on your first hop, cause it's such a shame when that happens." It might have been, "Luck."

I *zorched* out of the dining room. Quick stop in the head. Didn't take time to wash hands. Found a puddle of jet fuel on the flight deck to sanitize the hands. Preflight the jet.

The air boss announced, "Good afternoon, girls. The

temperature today is a balmy 120 degrees. You guys frying eggs on the catapult tracks, get the hell away from there. Start engines."

Checks completed. Ready to go. Signal thumbs-up. Just then, None walked out of the island and headed back toward his plane. The CO said his name was None, but I still wished, *Luck, Newbie.*

The midday go had a lot of planes on it. The flight deck crew was anxious to shoot me. And I was glad about that because, however hot it was outside my cockpit, it was a lot hotter inside. The A-4 air-conditioning system worked like a champ in the air, but not at all at idle power. With the canopy closed, even my fingernails and hair were perspiring. Sweat puddled in my oxygen mask, covering the exhalation port. Sweat bubbled out of the mask. Some of it got in my eyes. I could sort of see.

Kaboom. A cat shot on a hot day—it loosened your fillings. But I was flying. I got the gear up, unsnapped the oxygen mask, and dumped it out as I waited for enough knots to raise the flaps. I wiped the sweat out of my eyes, unlocked the seat harness so I could move, and settled down for a nice, peaceful aerial visit to Uncle Ho to deliver some five-hundred-pound communication devices—to him personally, I hoped. Flaps up. Accelerating nicely—300 knots. Peachy.

Kaboom. Something blew right behind me. My jet slowed, as if someone had put the brakes on. I was slowing down fast. The fire light glowed red and sucked my eyes to it. On fire. *Slowing!* I grabbed the ejection handle and jerked. *Kaboom.*

The ejection blacked me out. I came to maybe a couple hundred feet in the air, still strapped to the seat, which was tilted forward. I looked down at water coming up.

Get out of the seat.

It was supposed to happen automatically. Automatic things sometimes ain't. *Do it manually. Where in hell's the handle?* Oh, yeah. I reached for the seat release on the right. Before I got to it, I was free. But, below me, the water was still coming up fast.

The parachute was supposed to open automatically. *That handle is where?* Left shoulder. As I reached for it, the chute opened.

I bit my tongue. My feet hit the water. I went under. An instant later, I was on the surface, on my back, the chute dragging me.

It was just like in survival training. They hooked up a student pilot in a simulated parachute rig, threw him off the back of a boat, and dragged him. He had to get out of the chute straps. Then he was taught to swim clear of the chute so he wouldn't get entangled in the shroud lines. That day, I did it just like the training and paused a moment to say thanks to the US Navy for the training and to apologize for calling it a dipshit, useless, meaningless way for old farts to torture young ones.

Clear of the chute, I pulled the toggle to inflate my floatation gear. The bladder around my waist puffed out. I hung still in the water a moment, about to take a breath, the first one in a long time it seemed. Fortunately, I noticed my mouth and nose were still under water. Something was wrong with the floatation gear. It should have supported me with my chin above the surface.

Note to the reader: You may have noticed it's been a while since I mentioned None. He'll be back. I'm telling this how it happened. It has a bearing on how come some of him stuck to my soul that day.

Treading water sucked energy out of me so fast I had a clear view of how little I had to burn. A plastic box of survival equipment strapped to my butt weighed me down. I undid the lap buckles securing the gear to me. It didn't help.

Oxygen mask. I always slipped the hose of mine through my harness, which attached me to the ejection seat. We were not supposed to do that because of the exact situation I was in right now. The mask attached to a small bottle of oxygen in the survival pack to sustain life in the event of a high-altitude ejection. In my case, I was in water and needed to rid myself of the weight of the survival gear. If my hose had not been run through the harness, the mask would have pulled free, and I'd have floated higher. But one of the things that happened in the A-4 aircraft was that a pilot sometimes got his oxygen hose tangled around the canopy-opening handle. If the canopy opened in flight, the wind stream could catch the seat-firing handle. I did not want to be over North Vietnam, jerking spastically around in the cockpit to look for SAMs and MiGs, accidently lose my canopy, and then get ejected for an all-expenses paid vacation in the Hanoi Hilton. As an FNG, I'd decided to worry more about the Hanoi Hilton than drowning. It had seemed like a good idea at the time. So my fingers trailed my oxygen hose down to where it plugged into the top of the survival pack, and I unhooked it.

Voila! My chin rose above the surface. I sucked in a massive gulp of air.

Wait! I'd been right in front of the carrier when I punched out. *God, did You bring me through all this just to run my ass over with an aircraft carrier? Laughing Your divine butt off are You?* I spun around to a most glorious sight. The carrier was turning. I wasn't going to be run over.

Thank You, God. Um, that other stuff I was saying to You ...

Rotor blades *whop-whopped* behind me. A swimmer jumped out of the helo, hooked me up to a harness, and the two of us were hauled up and into the jiggly comfort of the womb inside the rescue bird. Never again would I say, "A helicopter doesn't fly. It is so ugly, it's rejected by earth"—well, like the captain on H.M.S. *Pinafore,* "Hardly ever."

I rode the helo for another fifteen minutes while the ship completed launching the strike. Then it landed. After I'd deplaned, a flight surgeon handed me an airline-size bottle of Jim Beam. I figured I had been Joe Cool through my entire experience. A survival situation had come up. Calmly, I'd assessed; calmly, I'd acted. Another situation, more calm assessment, more calm action. Joe Cool, for sure. Except my hand shook so badly, I never got one drop of that luscious whiskey close to my mouth. Some situations turn FOGs into FNGs.

I wound up in a bed in sick bay. My neck hurt. Nothing on X-ray, but you know how quacks are. They wanted to watch me for a bit. So I lay there while this kind of 8 mm movie played over and over in my head—the cat shot, the kabooms, the water, what I'd said to God, the helo.

During the seventeenth rerun, Combat Fats rushed in and said, "Bad news, man. None was shot down."

"The FNG? On his first hop! I wish—I don't know what the hell I wish," I moaned.

Fats left.

I thought about None. Normally, new guys got the call sign Newbie, but the CO had pronounced his name. I wished we'd have given him the normal Newbie name. When you lost a newbie, he hadn't been around long. In many cases, the CO hadn't even categorized him ass-kick-wise. But a guy named None!

I looked up at heaven, the overhead festooned with cables, and prayed. *What the hell, God? Couldn't You pick on somebody other than a newbie just once?*

Combat Fats rushed back in. "It wasn't None," he said. "It was your roommate. TML was shot down."

TML had a very long last name. We called him Too Many Letters. TML.

Combat told me to hang in there—that guys from the squadron would be down to see me soon.

He rushed out.

"Corpsman," I hollered. "Where's my damn flight suit?"

"Sir, the doc says you should stay overnight."

"Flight suit!"

"I have to call the doc."

The thirteen-year-old-by-appearance, skinny, bepimpled corpsman grabbed the black phone off the desk and dialed. His back was to me.

I left, barefoot and in skivvies. The nonskid coating on the hangar deck was not fun to walk on without shoes. People looked at me tender-footing around planes and equipment on the way to my, now, one-man room. On a carrier in the Gulf of Tonkin, sometimes you saw stuff like me. No way did I want to stay in sick bay and talk to the guys. I felt like I had made a deal with God and traded TML for the FNG.

None and May 27 bloomed vividly, not so much in memory, but in my soul.

May 28 had been a no-fly day on our carrier, which I needed, but I would never have admitted that to anyone. On the twenty-ninth, the schedule listed me for two hops over the North. On the first one, I made a very interesting discovery. I could turn my head to the left, no problem; but turn that sucker to the right, and I felt see-nothing-but-white-light, butt-muscles-pucker-so-hard-they-suck-grommets-out-of-the-seat-pad *pain*. It hurt like hell. Fortunately, no Commies came from my right side. Of course, if a navy pilot can only turn his head in one direction, left is the way he'd choose to have it. To land on a carrier in the day, a pilot executes a left turn.

I got back to the ship and asked the schedules officer to give me nothing but tanker hops for a couple of days, which he did.

After two days, the pain went away, and I flew with None. In the brief, I was impressed with his focus, his attention. On his face, I could see he was taking aboard every item being discussed. I remember thinking, *If more FNGs paid attention like that, more of them would live to be FOGs.*

In the air, every time I looked for him, predisposed to cuss the FNG for being out of position, he wasn't. None was a good stick.

A month later, we went into port. In the midst of the hooting and hollering, there was None. He participated perfectly appropriately. As a lieutenant (junior grade) and an FNG, he seemed to be mindful of his station and to sense the proper line to walk without wallowing into deference. It was a law of nature: FOGs did not admire FNGs. But None had something I admired. I didn't know what to call it at the time. Twenty years later, after seeing the Clint Eastwood movie, *In the Line of Fire,* I did know what to call it. In the movie, the bad guy does his evil with panache.

None had subcutaneous panache. It was there. You just had to look for it. Later on, I can't remember when, I found out None played the oboe; and he played it well. I had met guitarists, pianists, banjoists, bassists, organists, trumpeters, buglers, drummers, sopranos, baritones, a hammer dulcimer player, an organ grinder monkey, and a musical armpit band. But None was my one and only oboist. He told me about the movie *The Mission* and the score, which rides on "Gabriel's Oboe." I have the movie on VHS. When I play it, my ears pay way more attention than my eyes do. I love that score.

Years after None told me about "Gabe's Oboe," my wife's choral group performed "Nella Fantasia," which is lyrics set to "Gabriel's Oboe." I wound up recording the choral group's performances with a video camera and putting it on a DVD. Thinking None might appreciate "Nella Fantasia," I sent him a copy. Not long after, None sent me a CD he and a few of his buds had recorded in his kitchen. Christmas music mostly, but one track was "Gabriel's Oboe."

The e-mail forward brought all that back in a big throat-lumping ball of jumbled musical emotion—None, "Gabriel's Oboe," *The Mission*, "Nella Fantasia" performed by Sister Joan's Carondolet Women's Choral Group in a wondrous blend of voices with mature range and timbre, and "Nella Fantasia" performed by Jackie Evancho on *America's Got Talent* in an angelic voice of such crystal purity and innocence you couldn't imagine that voice ever having said a cross word. And all of that rode on what None had told me about "Gabriel's Oboe." There was a depth to the man.

An oboist for crap sake.

Another thing the e-mail forwards triggered was a reminder of the greatest trick anyone had ever pulled on me. *The* greatest.

It was 1992. I was on my second-to-last assignment before retiring, which I didn't know. At the time, I had no idea they didn't want me to be chief of Naval Operations. Anyway, I had been stationed at SHAPE (Supreme Headquarters Allied Powers Europe) for two years when None joined the staff.

SHAPE was located in the French-speaking part of Belgium. I began French lessons right after checking aboard. For two years, I slogged through audio and VHS tapes. Still, every time I opened my mouth in a Parisian shop, the salesperson's face assumed a look, which I was sure meant: *After all this time, why hasn't someone invented a palate cleanser for the ears?*

So after None showed up, a mutual buddy, Bruce, an army colonel who'd been to the US Defense Department language school and jabbered French into French ears that were happy to be jabbered into, invited None, Amanda Sue, my wife, and me to go to a French restaurant with him and his wife. We met at Bruce's house for cocktails first.

After providing us with beverages, Bruce said to me, "You've been studying French. I heard this song on the radio the other day. The lyrics are really simple. I bet you'll understand them. And it's a cool song. You'll like it. I'll play a line, okay?"

"Sure." What the heck. It couldn't be as bad as the shops in Paris.

Bruce played a line of the song, stopped the tape, and looked at me expectantly.

The only thing I understood sounded like "Les Ricans." A French song about Puerto Ricans, maybe? "No, man. I don't have a clue."

Bruce played it again. I still didn't get it.

"Wait," None said and rattled off a phrase, English translating the French.

Bruce smiled. "Great, None. The *Les Ricans* part means *The Americans,* in a hip jargon way. The rest of the line you got what the song said."

I was not pleased. I'd been studying the language for two years. None had been at it six weeks. I glared at None. He shrugged apologetically.

"Let me play the next line. I'm sure you'll get this one," Bruce assured me.

He played it. I didn't get it. None did. It went that way the next two lines of the song.

After None gave us the translation of the fourth line, I was frosted and stood up intending to pour my beer on him. None turned his bottle and showed me the back of it. Attached to his Stella Artois was a sticky note with the translated lyrics. Bruce laughed. None laughed. I blushed. The women felt bad for me. I stopped being mad and felt bad for me too.

They got me good. Bruce and None played their parts *magnifiquement*. After twenty-two years, I am able to appreciate the orchestration of the prank without clenching my jaw and cracking fillings and crowns.

That e-mail forward, the way it brought None back, it was almost a resurrection.

Like many of us, he was blessed with a better half. So, an Amanda Sue story to round this out. None and Amanda Sue lived in an apartment in Meridian, Mississippi, while he went through basic jet training. A number of other student pilots abided in the same complex. One weekend, None decided to host a party at their place. He'd been to parties in some of the bachelors' pads and had decided a cleaned-recently venue was more conducive to a good time. The better half raised an eyebrow when he proposed the soiree, which he took to be assent. The night of the grand whoop-de-do, the party was into the next morning when Amanda Sue suggested to the host that his invitees should be invited to leave. None nodded, intending to work on that task, but the party roared at Mach 2, and he got swept up in the mood.

Another spousal prod, a little later, to pull the plug on the party came his direction.

"Yeah. I will." None's promise was sincerely rendered.

Another bit later, a pounding on the door outshouted the celebration inside, followed by, "Open up. Police!"

Which created the sound of silence.

None opened the door and backpedaled, although he didn't move from the doorway. "Yes, officer. No, officer. Sorry, officer."

The partiers filed out. With a last threatening glower, the police departed. None closed the door. He turned to Amanda Sue.

"I wonder who called the police?" None asked. "Everybody who lives here was at the party."

An angelic smile illuminated Amanda Sue's face. "I did," she said.

My roommate TML spent nine months as a POW. He came home messed up physically. He was determined to make it back onto flight status and had plenty of hardheaded cussedness to get him there. I never told him he wouldn't have been a POW if I hadn't traded him for None. As they used to say in the bars of Olongapo, "Sorry 'bout that."

Which I only know because I heard guys talking.

Since the e-mail forward came, all kinds of thoughts tried to elbow their way into my head. Did God think TML was tough enough to handle POWdom, whereas None, being an FNG, maybe he needed a little more seasoning? Well, the Lord works in mysterious ways.

And I've thought about how other navy acquaintances' deaths have affected me. In the past, someone I served with passed away, and I wouldn't hear of it for years. When I did find out, it elicited a "too bad." That's how it had been on the carriers. After a maiming injury, a death, it was "Suck it up, girls. We got planes to launch." We launched 'em.

Maybe when you die, your spirit has to do things before it can leave earth. Maybe it has to run around the world and collect all those bits of itself Velcroed or sticky noted to the souls of those whose lives it touched. Maybe if you knew a person died, you'd know to hang onto the bits of people's souls stuck to you.

Maybe it's another way when you die.

Maybe I've gotten sentimental in my decrepitude.

What I do know is that e-mail forward saved something of None here on earth.

So, Lips, thanks for the original, and Combat Fats, thanks for the forward.

No man is an island.

All this time, I'd thought I was.

Voices†

When the silent majority speaks for you, it is hard as hell to hear what they are saying.

Maybe I have too much time to think right now. Maybe nobody ought to have this much time to think.

I almost died, a handful of times. Five times. About right I think. Four in an airplane. Actually if you count the time I ejected, I almost died six times. Let's not make this overly complicated. I almost died four times in airplanes. There. That's settled.

Once in our big, blue Chevy van, I almost died and took five kids along with me. I was merging from I-5 South onto the lane connecting to the bridge over San Diego Bay to Coronado. I remember how there was another lane merging right there and how there was a big blind spot at the right rear of our van. So I turned to check the blind spot as I slipped into the turn lane. When I faced front again, there was this weensy Porsche convertible stopped dead in front of me. A guy with a ball cap sat behind the wheel, a blond ponytail next to him. I could have crushed them, but I didn't want to kill anyone that day. I cut hard to the right, hoping I might smash into a guardrail. I'd probably ruin some cars, but hopefully, I wouldn't kill anyone. Except there was no guardrail. The van knocked over a "Merging Traffic" sign, went over the edge of the curb, and barreled down this really steep embankment. It could have been a cliff, but it wasn't. At the bottom was a four-lane street. It could have been packed with cars, school buses maybe. But the street was devoid of vehicular occupation.

At the bottom of the slope, we were bouncing up and down vigorously. Chevy put good springs on those vans. I cut the wheel to the left and stopped at the stoplight, which was red. No big deal, right? The kids, three of them your sisters; one Chrissy, Jessica's friend; and a neighbor girl were all screaming at the top of their adolescent lungs.

"You wanna' do it again?" I asked.

The 120 dB screaming ceased. We passed a tick and a tock in silence.

Then "No!" which could have tumbled the walls of Jericho, blasted from the rear seats.

But that was almost dying. The real thing facing me now, it's weird. I guess I feel like a person ought to be able to practice—dying I mean. At any rate, the real thing is different from the almost dying bit. And right now, I can't tell you if it's a good thing to absolutely know it's coming or if I'm getting an early start on all the purgatory time I've piled up.

I thought I should write this down, kiddo. Not sure if anybody will care, but nothing else to do.

Once upon a time—

Just kidding.

A lot of stuff roils around in my head these days. One minute, I'm chin-drooping maudlin. The next, I'm giddy as a kitty on catnip. An even keel, especially sailors ought to maintain an even keel.

Okay. Al's my name. I'm serious now.

I served in Vietnam, came home, and Americans called me Baby Killer. This is a government "by the people." I thought the government sent me to Nam to fight for it. When I came home, people and the government called me Baby Killer for doing what they sent me to do. I didn't need voices telling me I was a hero, but I sure didn't care for that Baby Killer characterization. The war ended with me still owing the navy three years of service. In those postwar years, servicemen and women traveled in civilian clothes. The brass didn't want us showing up at meetings with spit on our uniforms. I stuck my chin out and soldiered on. See what kind of time it was, where even sailors had to soldier on?

They built the Wall. Every time I went to DC, I visited it. I still don't know what to think of those slabs of etched, black marble. When I stand there, in the weighty stillness of the place, I feel connected to those who died and those of us who served and lived. But why was the Wall erected? Did someone feel bad about the Baby Killer business? Lots of people seem to extract some kind of healing from the Wall. I never got that. Just things to wonder about. Why was the first monument to war dead in the capital for a war we lost?

I'd always admired World War II vets. If pressed to explain why, I don't think I could. There was no reason for me getting choked up over "The Star-Spangled Banner," either, but I always did. Then Tom Brokaw wrote that book. *The Greatest Generation* salted my wounds.

Stake out a greatest, it spotlights the other end of the spectrum too. A person just has to turn his head a mite to see *The Worst Generation.*

Baby Killers.

The greatest generation.

Tom Brokaw became their voice. He spoke to us about them, for them.

Lots of people have spoken for them and about them. One of the authors I've followed—read everything he published—is

James Lee Burke. In his *Wayfaring Stranger*, on page 26 of the hardcover, he writes about the generation who fought World War II as the last generation "to believe in the moral solvency of the Republic." I admire Mr. Burke—have since the first book of his I read. But I quibble with his *last generation to believe*. I was born in 1941. I think a lot of Americans born at the time I was felt as I did—that the United States of America was the greatest nation, the best form of government the human race had yet devised. And yes, it was still screwed up in places, but it would fix itself.

Voices have always swirled around—yours, theirs, his, hers, mine. It's the first-person, plural possessive pronoun I have trouble hooking onto the word *voice*. Our voice. *Their* voice called us the name. Where was *our* voice?

Since the "age of reason" overtook me, voices have chiseled themselves onto my soul alongside all the sins my recording angel etches there. Early on, Momma's and the nuns' voices worked to minimize the labors of my spirit scribe. Pop's voice was as rough and callous as his hands. He didn't say much. When he did speak, it stuck.

I remember one particular, "Get up." Usually I slept until eleven on Saturday. My shift ran from noon until eight at Martin's Grocery Store.

"Get up, I said." Pop didn't like to say a thing twice. He drove us to the navy recruiter's office, and I signed the paper where he pointed. After boot camp and electronics technician school, I reported to a destroyer.

"Welcome aboard, son," my division chief said in a right friendly voice.

We went to sea, and I puked every time anything entered my stomach, including air. It happened the next underway period too.

"You, Boar Tit," the chief said. "Report to the mess deck. Maybe they'll find a use for you."

Fortunately, I had taken a test for a navy scholarship before I reported to the ship. Halfway through my second three-month stint peeling potatoes, I received orders to attend Purdue University as a Naval Enlisted Scientific Education Program (NESEP) student.

School started right after my nineteenth birthday. At the next election, in 1964, I'd be able to vote. I would add my own voice in the matter of picking our president. Studying news and politics, along with engineering, I heard voices hyping JFK and Camelot. The US Navy was paying me to go to college. A lot of people might consider that to be a modernized paradise, my own personal Camelot, but I didn't agree with those voices, either. I'd sold a major chunk of my soul for an education. I dreaded the payback after graduation and had no ownership of, or part in, those voices saying "Camelot." The way it turned out, use of that word died before the president did.

In the election of '64, I was not *for* either candidate. Neither one of them spoke for me, but I was more strongly *not for* LBJ. Goldwater scared people, and LBJ won with 61 percent of the vote.

Not long after, voices began shouting, "Hell no, we won't go," and, "The Vietnam War is immoral." Vietnam didn't seem any more immoral than any other war we'd fought. Didn't any of those shouters hear Krushchev's voice? "We will bury you." It seemed to me that, if your enemy says that to you, you better do something before clods start raining on the lid of your coffin. So I went to Vietnam. But, honestly, I went because I owed the navy for my college education. The first secretary of the Communist Party's threat, however, stamped moral righteousness on the effort to try to stop them from burying us without lobbing nukes at anyone.

The navy sent me to Nam on a destroyer. I still puked but not as often. The newspapers from home were delayed getting to us, but the protest they reported was not muted by either time or distance. In those protest voices, I heard more antiestablishment and anti-America than anti–anything else. That half a generation after mine spoke, but it did not, by God, shout their phrases for me. Those protest voices aroused a sense of duty to my country and my conscience. So I became antiprotest and decided to stay in the navy. Pilots were the ones taking the fight into North Vietnam. I applied for flight training.

After receiving wings, I went back to the Tonkin Gulf.

Even as a lieutenant, I could see I'd gotten myself into a screwed-up war—not immoral but majorly screwed up. Defense Secretary McNamara said, "We're not bombing them. We're communicating with them." He also announced, "It's a limited war." In my opinion, there's nothing limited about a war when you're flying through flak and dodging surface-to-air missiles. Ask the grunts how limited it was. Somewhere, way, way up the line, McNamara was my boss. But he sure as hell did not speak for me.

President Nixon made the phrase "silent majority" famous. Great! A silent voice might now be speaking for me. Even though he was elected with an even bigger landslide than LBJ had been, the protest voices grew louder and louder. It didn't take long. Nixon and the ephemeral notion of a silent majority went down in flames—just as Camelot had.

During Nam, I felt as if I were fighting the US military and political bureaucracy as much as the North Vietnamese and the Viet Cong. Ironic. The reason I became a career sailor was because of the antiestablishment protest. And what did I do? I raised my voice and fought the establishment. I flew my missions with a determination that I would not lose *my* part of the war. I didn't agree with target restrictions or many of the other Rules of Engagement. To me, the rules seemed to say, "Tie both hands behind your back. Now get in that boxing ring and give the other guy hell."

All told, I spent thirty-six years in the navy. Most of that time, I wound up disagreeing with the voices around and above me. I spoke up and said things like "Why can't we fix this?" and "Why don't we try it this way?" and "Don't you see how stupid this is?"

It earned me a lot of "What the hell were you thinking when you said …?"

There must have been some supportive voices. Otherwise, they'd never have let me stay for three and a half decades. The supportive voices were the silent kind, though.

Presidents came and went. Causes that united people into raising their voices came and went. Only once did I claim a share in a national voice. President Ronald Reagan and his supporters spoke *for* me. All those other voices spoke *to* me, and mostly down to me. Of course, Reagan's voice lasted only eight years.

My president left office, and I figured I wouldn't live long enough to hear another national voice I could attach a personal possessive pronoun to.

After I got out of the navy, I worked for an aerospace company for eleven years, and spent as much time away from home as I had in the service. I liked my job, saved diligently, and looked forward to a second retirement. Finally, I'd be able to spend some time with Angela, the woman I'd married forty-four years prior.

I reretired. Two months later, Angela's doctor discovered stage 4 ovarian cancer. How the hell could Angela die first? It didn't seem possible.

Before she passed, I thought I'd pretty much run through life alone. I mean she was right there beside me, and she heard, "What the hell were you thinking?" every time I did. They hurt her more than me. What I did was take her for granted. I didn't really appreciate the treasure she was until she was gone, and I discovered what real "alone" was.

A couple of weeks after we buried her, circulation to my digestive tract quit—just quit. Doctors explained it. They'd explained Angela's demise as well, but the explanation didn't matter beyond she got cancer; she died. Me? Blood stopped flowing to my guts. IVs kept me alive.

So, Jennifer, I don't really know why I'm writing these notes for you. I'm almost finished. Every day, I lie in my hospital bed and stare at the ceiling. I think about bacon. It doesn't even smell good anymore. Once that's gone, why would a man want to go on? I think about those voices that called me a baby killer after Nam. All these years, I rejected being labeled such. But you know, when I punched the bomb pickle aiming at a truck on the Ho Chí Minh trail, I was a mile up. I had no idea whether there was a baby in an infant seat next to the driver or not. Maybe I did kill babies. But the truck carried bullets so the Viet Cong could kill our soldiers and marines. It's taken a long time, but thinking about being called Baby Killer no longer makes my jaws clamp and my teeth grind. The other thing I think about is pulling the plug. All I have to do is decide. Tell them to pull it. Just decide. Just say it. Sounds easy. But I can't say it. Not just yet.

Jennifer, our first child, came every evening at 1900.

Two minutes after seven … Where the hell was she?

I heard voices in the hall. Six guys trooped into my room and surprised the hell out of me. It was Wart, Butt Chin, Skunk, Dog Lips, Brain Dead, and VD, guys I'd flown with in Nam. They stayed twenty minutes.

Then five guys from my carrier tour filed in. My exec, my

OPS-O, my air boss, my command master chief, and a black man who was younger than the other old farts. I didn't recognize him.

"Seaman Apprentice Cassidy," he said with a big grin.

I had taken him to captain's mast twenty years before and told him, "You can make something out of yourself, Cassidy, or you can go to an early grave or prison. You're at a fork in the road. Decide which path you want to take."

"I did go to prison," Mr. Cassidy said. "But I went with a counseling degree. I've been rehabilitating criminals for eight years. Got me a real nice 'fork in the road' speech I lay on 'em."

The next visitors consisted of two men and two women from the program I worked my last years at Boeing.

They left, and Jennifer came in. Her eyes were red.

"Why are you crying?"

"Your voices!" she sobbed and grabbed more Kleenexes.

"Our voices?"

She nodded and blew her nose.

"Our voices."

I reached for her hand. She squeezed it. Her brown eyes were Angela's.

"Half of me is tubes, hoses, and bags."

She tried real hard not to totally lose it. I could feel her pain, but I also felt my face smile.

"Our voices," I said.

She let go of my hand, blew her nose again, went into the bathroom to deposit her handful of tissues, came out, and grabbed more Kleenexes from the box on the rolling tray.

So, Jennifer, I'll wrap up this letter, this confession. It is a confession. I had this Baby Killer thing stuck in my belly for four decades. It made me a bitter old poop, and I am heartily sorry for it. Your mother used to tell me to just let it go or to give it to God. I couldn't let go. I felt that if I did, the middle of me would disintegrate. My arms and legs would drop to the ground, and my head would roll down the hill. And I knew it for an ugly thing. I couldn't give it to God. So I hung on to it—until last night.

What you did, rounding all those people up to visit, I can't say thanks enough for that. Somewhere in all that hooting and hollering and after, when you came in and said, "Your voices," well, I don't know exactly what happened, but I feel like I'm cured of bitter-old-poop-ness.

We did a fine thing for the world, your mother and me, when we made you. The earth is way overdue for another great generation.

See you later, kiddo,

Dad

PS. I am reconciled to the Baby Killer thing, but please don't let them put that on my tombstone. Okay?

Author's Note

As noted on the contents page, versions of two of these stories have been previously published. I completed a version of "The Noble Guerilla" a couple of years ago. Then I had a recommendation to turn the story into a novel-length work, which I am working on. It will be called *Guerilla Bride*. The germ of the story for "The Short, Happy Love Life of Heiny Bauer" was lifted from chapter 12 of *Noble Deeds*, which was published in 2013. I thought the tale would work as a short story. Further, I have always admired Hemingway's "The Short Happy Life of Francis Macomber," and I wanted to try a story like it. Bits of "Newbie" and "Darling, Daddy, Dead Vietcong Maker" appear in *The Junior Officer Bunkroom*, which was published in 2015. Working on all these *short* stories has been interesting and challenging, "The Free Upgrade" particularly so. I completed the story several years ago. Two years ago, I came across an ad soliciting entries for a "Missouri Liars Contest." Entries had to be either audio or video files (with sound track of course). I decided to try the "Free Upgrade" story on them. I submitted an MP3 file and was chosen to be a finalist in a lie-off. Well, I didn't win, but it was an interesting exercise. Packaging the tale for verbal delivery, vice the printed page, I wound up altering the narration considerably when I listened to early versions of my submittal file. Intentional disregard of tenses and grammar, at times, I thought, enhanced the narration. I absolved myself of any guilt over such sins since it was for a gathering of liars.

Printed in the United States
By Bookmasters